Rum
to the
Reggae

LYNN JOSEPH

For my rum and reggae lovers everywhere.

Chapter One

The blue boat rises and falls before smacking into a wave. Salty water dashes across the bow and drenches me with rainbow-colored drops.

"Is it supposed to do that?" I shout over the sound of the engine.

Keston Kips grins widely. "If we want to win, yes. It does that and more."

As if testing out the "more," he pushes the throttle forward and the boat skips over the waves like a dancing porpoise.

"We might die before we win," I grumble.

He shakes his head. "We haven't died yet."

"Exactly. No need to test fate."

But he doesn't hear me because another boat plows through the sea next to us, sending up a giant wave of water.

"Damn you, Starr," Keston shouts at the giant fisherman in his mid-thirties, whose dark muscles upon muscles make him look like a Black Thor. His boat, *Ghost Rider*, roars off, leaving a wake of white water.

The wave would swamp us if not for Keston's quick sideways maneuver that throws me off balance and into his solid, muscled chest.

He holds the steering wheel with one hand, the throttle with the other, and still manages to bend down and kiss me on my lips.

"You okay, baby? I'm sorry. They came out of nowhere."

"Thank God I'm wearing a life jacket. The only one in this madcap scavenger hunt to be doing so."

"The fishermen of St. Nicholas believe they're invincible. Probably from years of doing a hazardous job."

"You guys are nuts," I shout into the wind. "I can't believe you do this 'Pirate Regatta' every year." I hold up the laminated list of items we're in a race to collect from all over the island by boat only.

We're supposed to beg, borrow, steal, or kidnap the items in honor of the pirate theme. No legitimate buying is allowed.

I wouldn't know where to purchase the tail feather of a frigate bird or a shell from the bottom of Mermaid Pool, even if we *could* buy them.

"Aren't you glad you're here for this?" Keston beams so brightly that I can't throw cold water on his enthusiasm. Even though we're getting sloshed by gallons of saltwater as a fisherman with an apparent death wish spins 360s in *Call Me Crazy* at high speed.

Fear charges through me from head to toe. He could easily hit our boat.

"This is so dangerous. Am I the only person who thinks we should have some basic rules for this competition?"

"*Rules?*" Keston says as if he had never heard the word before.

"Like not endangering lives. That could be Rule No. 1."

He chuckles, "Wait until you see the cliff divers."

I blink. "Cliff divers?" I eye the emerald-green hills. Shadowy rocks demarcate the bottoms of the cliffs like a Bob Ross painting.

I shudder. "I can't *wait* for that."

He grins at me like a little kid with a new toy. His blue powerboat is that toy.

Keston worked hard all month to get it ready for today.

Ever since I arrived on St. Nicholas to reunite with the man I realized I was in love with, Keston has started working on "projects," as he calls them.

It was like he got a new lease on life when I showed up.

I'm happy to inspire and motivate, but I never imagined the old dirty shell of a boat sitting upside down in his beach backyard would look like this flying blue bird.

With newly upholstered side-by-side console seats cushioned in marine stripes, a giant, noisy engine he and a mechanic tinkered with for one whole week, to the point where I almost offered to buy him a new engine (but now am glad I didn't), and a steering wheel as big as the one in my Mom's Tahoe back in upstate New York.

Keston did a whole Grease Lightning transformation on this vessel.

All he'd talked about was how much I'd love the "Pirate Regatta."

But now that I'm here, risking my life and spitting out mouthfuls of seawater, I'm having second thoughts. His idea of fun and mine are totally different.

I'd be happy lounging under a coconut tree with a good book. Not galloping wildly over waves and dodging kamikaze boats.

"What's the prize again?" I ask, squinting through the spray of water hosing our boat. What he told me last week doesn't seem like it's worth all this trouble.

"A bottle of rum."

"That's it?"

"An *old* bottle of rum."

"What's so great about that?"

He gives me a side-eye. "Aged rums have more character. They're complex. Served great neat, on the rocks, *and* in cocktails."

"How old are we talking?"

"The older the better." He pops a kiss on my forehead. "Like you."

I swat his arm. "Rude!"

He laughs, turning the steering wheel on our power boat hard to the left to navigate what looks like an underwater shelf of rocks.

"Aren't you afraid you'll hit a rock or something?" I ask.

He shakes his head confidently. His dark, curly hair is held back off his face by a bandana in rasta colors. His curls shimmer with drops of seawater.

With broad shoulders that easily carry two full buckets of water from the spring near his beach house, sparkling brown eyes that look at me as if I'm the only woman in the world, a toothpaste white smile, and an optimistic attitude that rivals a giant purple dinosaur's, Keston Kips is not exactly the type of man I imagined I'd fall for.

But he's everything I want and need.

Which makes him perfect for me.

A thought that usually has me smiling inside and out.

Except for times like now. When I worry if our incredibly different lifestyles will wreak havoc on our relationship. Maybe even be a deal breaker.

I'm a New York lawyer who loves her daily planners, her daily structure, and having brunch with my girlfriends at new restaurants on the weekends.

As unromantic as that sounds, it's how I was raised; it's who I am.

Keston is the opposite of me. He's an island man who catches, cleans, and cooks his own food. Most of his time is spent outside, and other than his job as a mixologist at Cocoa Reef Resort, he has no planned activities.

He lives for today. Let tomorrow take care of itself. That's his motto.

Living on this gorgeous island should be easy, except I'm struggling with the see-what-happens attitude.

When I returned to St. Nicholas with a six-week plan to see if I could live here with Keston, I didn't expect to confront so many lifestyle changes.

"What are you thinking about, sweetheart?" Keston nudges my leg with his.

His skin is hot. It reminds me of the heat he brings under the sheets.

When I don't answer right away, he frowns, looking sincerely worried. "Are you feeling seasick? Should we stop?"

The fact that he'd give up his fun and games in a second *for me* silences any relationship doubts.

What am I thinking? Keston Kips loves me to the moon and back. I am a very lucky woman.

"Nothing's wrong, my love. Let's win this thing."

The smile that splits his face is entirely for me. A thank you, and I love you wrapped up in one.

How could I ever believe we might end?

Keston's boat does not have a name.

When he finished painting it with a blue gel coat a few days ago he said he wanted to name it after me.

He started throwing out hilarious monikers like "CJ's Nauti by Nature" and "CJ's a Knotty Girl."

"You'll give everyone the idea that I only want you for sex," I said.

"And I'd be wrong?" His eyebrows twitched at me. "How about CJ's Bouy Toy?"

I smacked his arm. "You'll ruin my reputation. They already think I'm some cougar."

He rolled his eyes. "Like we care what anyone thinks?"

"I'm trying to make a good impression, Kes. It's a small island. If I'm going to live here, I need to become an upstanding resident."

"First of all, it's 'when', not 'if.' Second, you want to know what's upstanding? Feel this." He pointed at his shorts, where a giant bulge poked out.

I stuck my hands behind my back. "Nuh-uh."

He looked sadly at the erection threatening to bust out. "Buddy, she's not interested right now. Sorry."

"I didn't say *that*." My eyes were riveted on the ridge in his shorts; I couldn't lie.

A slow sexy smile graced his lips. He started counting on his fingers.

Had he forgotten about his erection?

He glanced up where the sun shone merrily down on us from the cobalt blue sky that matched the sea.

"It has been five whole hours since you ripped my shirt off."

I choked on a laugh. I am not a cheery person by nature, but Keston Kips cracks me up even when I don't want to laugh.

"You haven't worn a shirt all day," I pointed out. "Plus, we can't go around spending all our time in bed."

"Who said anything about a bed?" His brown eyes gleamed wickedly.

He patted the brand-new cushions in the boat. "We can at least christen our vessel, even if we're not naming it yet."

He pulled me into his arms. Started kissing my neck, running his hands up and down my body.

He has the amazing ability to relax and excite me at the same time.

His callused fingers found their way inside my silky Victoria's Secret shorts.

"*Oooh,*" I moaned as he caressed an ass cheek in one hand and stroked my pussy with the other.

His hard cock pushed against my soft mound, rubbing up and down on my shorts until I was soaking wet.

I was almost on the verge of coming but didn't want to yet.

I loved seeing what else he would do to my body. All the ways he could send me flying.

His mouth closed on my nipple, protruding through my silk chemise. He nipped, tugged, and teased it until I shivered from head to toe.

"Yes," I moaned. "Don't stop. Please don't stop."

It was like I had a live wire from my nipples to my clit.

His breath blew hot on my skin. "I won't ever stop, baby. You feel too good."

Pussy juices ran down my legs. It was a wonder all my panties weren't hanging on his clothesline.

My head lolled back. I closed my eyes to slow my orgasm.

"Not fair," I murmured. "I want to touch you too."

With one hand, he untied and dropped his shorts, releasing his beautiful, massive cock at full attention.

I gripped it as if I'd never let it go.

"You like it, baby? You want it?" he moaned. "Because it wants you."

"Uh-huh," I nodded, out of breath.

Another roaring orgasm was coming my way. My toes curled in the sand with anticipation.

"Fuck," I shouted as his fingers and mouth took me to great heights. My breathing was shallow. My pussy opened up in his hand.

"I'm coming," I shrieked.

Chapter Three

His mouth sucked hard on my nipples as his fingers kneaded my clit with just the right amount of pressure.

It was like a waterfall hitting all the right spots.

The sound of my scream echoed across the trees. Birds took flight. It would be embarrassing if it weren't so earth-shattering.

The joy I felt under Keston's generous lovemaking was unbeatable.

"That was so good," I sighed. My hand still held onto his cock. It throbbed and leaked precum.

He smiled. "Now, be a good girl, and let's pull down those cute shorts. The boat needs to be christened."

"Here?" I asked. "In the yard. You want to have sex in broad daylight?"

Keston scoffed. "What do you think we've been doing? Playing chess?"

"Suppose someone drives up?"

"It's a private road. There's no one around but us."

I glanced around.

"This is not the time to get paranoid, missy. Not after *that* performance."

I smacked his arm. "Why can't we go inside?"

"Woman, turn around. Our boat is waiting. Not to mention this one-eyed monster here."

I giggled. "You're so corny."

"And you love it."

"Yes, I do," I admitted.

I decided to be brave like him and tossed off my clothes.

I did a ballerina twirl, completely naked. His appreciative grin gave me the confidence to twirl again. With him, I forget I'm forty years old.

"You're bad for me," I grumbled. "You're turning me into an exhibitionist."

"Good. As long as I'm the only one in the audience." He smacked my ass playfully before bending me over the edge of the refurbished boat.

With the sea right at his front door and the rainforest all around us, I stuck my ass in the air. "If you can't beat them . . ." I laughed.

"You fuck them," he said, sliding his thick cock into my soaking pussy. He took his time so it wouldn't hurt too much. But it always does.

He whistled. "Nice, tight pussy you got, baby. It was made for me."

I grabbed each ass cheek and spread them to make room for his big dick. It was like letting a bull into a china shop. Things were gonna get messed up.

And sure enough, he grabbed my hips, pumping his dick in and out of my pussy, making loud squelching noises.

"Woman," he growled, panting to the finish line, "you are mine."

I couldn't disagree even if I wanted to.

"Okay, so what are we going to call her?"

We were lying in the shallow water, floating and holding hands so we wouldn't drift too far apart.

The sunblock I sprayed on made my skin glisten.

"I don't know, honey. It's your boat."

"Our boat. Like this is our beach. Our house. Our donkey."

"Our donkey? Do you mean the annoying animal that trots down the dirt road to your house in the wee hours of the morning, then brays along with the roosters crowing to wake us up? That donkey?"

He squeezed my hand. "It'll grow on you."

"Doubt that."

"How about calling the boat, '*True Love's Dream*?'"

I wrinkled my nose. "Too cheesy."

"*Ready for Love*?"

"Worse."

"Fine, you are in charge of naming our vessel."

I splashed water on his face. "What will we be using it for?"

He closed his eyes. I did, too, as the water caressed us like a warm bath.

"We can return to No Man's Land," he said. "To have those romantic picnics on the beach that you dreamed about when we were stranded."

"I'm not sure I'm ready to go back there." It was only six months ago that we were stuck on that deserted island and almost died!

"Well, it doesn't have to be tomorrow. We can visit the island where we fell in love any time you want. With a bottle of champagne."

"And a satellite phone?"

This time he splashed water on *my* face.

"Yes, silly. And a sat phone."

Chapter Four

The Pirate Regatta is one big party on the sea. In fact, it is more party, less pirate. It should be renamed the Party Regatta.

In every boat we pass, the captains and crew are laughing, singing along to music on their stereos, and drinking rum straight from the bottle.

From what I can tell, scavenging the items on the laminated lists seems to be a secondary concern. The fishermen are more interested in outmaneuvering each other's weathered boats with speed and tricks.

I stand with my feet spread wide, bracing against the ups and downs of the rolling waves. And the unexpected attack of a rival.

"This is madness. I get the feeling that you're not chugging rum like they are because I'm here."

Keston chuckles. "You're partly right. I stopped drinking like them while recovering from my injury. But I can always get back to it. To be like a real pirate."

"No thanks. I prefer my pirates in theory, not reality."

Keston leans forward as the boat leaps like a hurdler over a blue mini wall of water.

"Sit down, honey. It's going to get worse."

"Worse than this?"

Standing up and holding onto the dashboard seemed safer than a seat with no seatbelts.

But I decide to follow instructions. Just this once.

I plop down into the seat. "You should have seatbelts."

He presses one of his extremely muscled calves back against my legs. "Hold on to this."

I scoff. "Please. Just because I told you once that you possess the sexiest calves I've ever seen. Now I have to hear about them all the time."

He glances back at me. "I have other fine attributes."

Before I can respond, a rival boat, the *African Queen*, squeals up to ours. A man I know as Captain Shaq tosses something into our boat.

"Is that a fish?" I shriek. "Oh my God. It's alive." I pull my legs up off the floor.

The long, silvery fish flops about, gasping for air.

Keston doesn't slow down.

The rugged fisherman who doubles as a lifeguard at the beaches laughs like it's the biggest joke ever.

"Loverboy, you'll have to stop now!" yells Captain Shaq.

"Never!" Keston growls. "Watch your backs. That rum is mine!"

Keston sounds like a crazed pirate.

"Your New York lady won't touch that fish," Shaq shouts as Keston edges past his boat. "You'll have to stop." He salutes me, "Sorry, miss."

As we speed off, I hear the deep rumbles of laughter coming from other boats behind us.

"It's a setup," Keston grouses.

"You all are evil," I shout across the waves at the men I've come to know from going with Keston to buy fresh fish almost daily at the jetty in Roucou, the village nearest his home.

But all the fish we bought were filleted, wrapped in brown paper, and tied with string.

Not this flopping and flailing sea creature eyeballing me.

"I can't watch him die," I cry. "He's staring into my eyes. He knows death is close at hand."

"Close at hand?" Keston huffs. "What is this, a fairytale?"

"Help him, Keston. Don't let him die like this."

The boat churns through the waves. White water kicks up behind us in a giant spray.

I feel exactly like this fish. Out of my element.

Keston doesn't slow down.

"I'm not losing this race, CJ."

"I'm not watching that fish die!"

Part of me wonders what he'll do. It's a completely foreign situation for me. Even when we were stranded on No Man's Land, I didn't have to confront a large dying fish.

It's the same way I wondered last week what Keston would

do when the donkey showed up in his yard. It had ginormous teeth. It walked straight up the clothesline and dragged off my favorite sundress.

Keston had laughed at the donkey parading around with my dress over its eyes.

"Stop!" I shouted at the donkey. "Bring that back!"

I stayed on the porch because I didn't want to get too close to it.

Keston thought it was hilarious.

I swatted his arm. "Do something!"

The donkey turned and ran down the dirt road, still wearing my pink flowered sundress.

"He can't see. He'll have an accident." I couldn't understand why Keston found it so funny.

"It's a *she*."

"Like that's supposed to make me feel better?"

He shrugged. "She probably just wants to borrow your dress."

"Well, can you please get it back for me?" I pointed at the road to show him I meant right now!

He could barely stop laughing long enough to jump on his rusty motorbike.

I leaped on the back thinking it would be a fast and furious experience. Find the donkey, wheel the bike in front of it to stop its progress, and rescue the dress.

By the time we reached the donkey, a bunch of teenagers in school uniforms were laughing and taking pictures of the donkey in a pink dress on their phones.

Even Keston whipped out his phone and took a picture.

Part of me was mad everyone thought the donkey ruining a perfectly good dress was funny. The other part was worried I had to stop their fun. I didn't want to get a reputation of being a party pooper.

As the poor fish is gasping for its last breaths, I'm caught between similar conflicting feelings.

Part of me is mad the fishermen are playing practical jokes on me, and Keston won't slow down to do anything about it.

The other part is worried that Captain Shaq is right. I'm too much of a New Yorker to touch a live fish.

I expected some culture clashes but not over things like a donkey and a fish.

As if sensing my inner turmoil, Keston says, "You know when we catch fish, this is what happens to them, right? They die. We cook them. You eat it without complaint. But they die first."

I stare at the poor fish.

"That's a kingfish. It'll be delicious in a fish soup tonight."

Maybe it's imagining this pretty silvery fish all cut up that pulls me out of my shock.

I jump out of the boat seat, bend down, and grab the large fish with both hands by its tail. This isn't easy because the fish is heavy and slippery, and its tail has a spiky fringe.

I swing the fish hard and toss it over the side of the boat.

It leaps up and over a wave, flashes its tail at me, and disappears under the sea.

"Whew!" I exclaim, turning to smile broadly at Keston.

"I did it." I feel a sense of real pride in saving its life.

"There goes our dinner."

"Sorry. But if I'm going to eat fish, I don't want to have a stare-down with it first."

"I'm proud of you, sweetie," he cuddles my head to his chest. "I know that wasn't easy."

"Why didn't you slow down and do it yourself?"

"One, you can't slow down out here. The water is rough, and there are rocks everywhere. Two, I knew you could.

Remind me to reward you later." He licks his lips. Leans back and looks pointedly at my breasts.

"You are horrible."

"Oh yeah? Tell me that tonight."

Damn! My nipples are hardening under his bold stare. I cross my arms. "Just drive the boat."

Ten minutes later, Keston weaves the vessel between towering craggy rocks. White birds roosting in crevices squawk at us.

I shut my eyes. "We're going to die."

"Don't be silly."

I peek to see Keston weaving the boat in and out of the

towering rock spires, maneuvering through the imposing stone giants that loom high above the water.

"Oh my God. We're going to hit one of those giant thingies."

"Rocks?"

"That's bigger than a rock. They're almost mountains. In the middle of the sea."

"We call them rocks."

"Very funny, pay attention."

"Geez, woman. I've been boating here all my life. We're not going to hit anything. Unless you jinx us."

That shuts me up. I cover my mouth with my hands in case I'm tempted to say any more.

I brace myself internally and outwardly for a massive crash. Which never comes.

"It's a shortcut. The other boats can't come this way."

"Can't or won't? Maybe they're smarter than I thought. Unlike *you*!"

"Whoa, CJ. You gotta have faith. I'm not crashing our boat. At least not until we name it."

The boat engine slows to a gentle murmur. Rough, calloused hands cover my arms, hugging me close to warm skin.

"Open your eyes all the way, baby. This is the best part."

I cautiously peek between my fingers.

"No faith," he fake grumbles.

I drop my hands and feel my mouth falling wide open.

Our boat sits in the middle of a clear, turquoise, sunlit pool. Rainbow-colored fish peck at the white sand below.

"But we're in the middle of the sea. How can the water be so clear and so shallow in this spot?"

"St. Nicholas is surrounded by reefs. With secret havens like this. Which is why pirates loved to hide out on this island."

"But what is this called?"

"Welcome to Mermaid Pool," Keston says dropping the small butterfly anchor onto a clear sandy patch.

Everything that felt as if it was going wrong today has been righted.

"This is breathtaking." I blink hard.

Keston swoops me up in his arms. "You ready to go dive for the mermaid shell?"

"Me?" I blubber.

He reaches under the console and hands me a dive mask and snorkel. Then, he pulls off his bandana and yanks down his mask over his head.

"Us! It'll always be us. Try to remember that."

"Us," I repeat, letting the short but meaningful word sit on my tongue.

As I shake out my curls and twist the mask into place, Keston scans the bottom of the pool. "It's pretty shallow. Less than fifteen feet."

"Okay," I say, unsure what that has to do with me. I'm not going any further than sticking my face in the water.

"Are we doing this?" he asks. "Before they catch up?"

"Yes," I say, settling the mask. "Let's do this."

Excitement grips me. I'm in a make-believe setting. A place for mermaids, it seems.

I have this hunk of a man at my side saying we'll always be an "us."

I grip the edge of the boat to leap over the side. I can't wait to get into the gorgeous, shimmering blue ripples.

Keston takes my hand. Kisses my knuckles and looks into my eyes behind my mask.

"Woman, why do I love you so much?" Without waiting for an answer, he says, "On three?"

"Wait," I shout. "Go back to how you love me so much."

But too late. Keston sings out, "One, two, three!"

And we leap.
Fingers entwined.
Right into the magical Mermaid Pool.
Maybe the Universe is trying to tell me something.
Keston and I are in this thing together.
Not only the race but this thing called life.

Keston and I pull up to the jetty at the end of the race and discover we're in *last* place.

"Last?" Keston asks incredulously.

The head of the event is a gorgeous woman. She's clocking in the boats with a stopwatch.

Her beauty stuns me speechless. I thought women like her

— tall, toned, honey-colored skin, honey-colored hair, green eyes, and two perfect dimples in her half-smile were only found in movies or magazine covers.

Not standing around in a white swimsuit, a floaty cape-like cover-up, and gold sandals emceeing a boat race on a tiny island.

"Who's that?" I whisper to Keston.

He's frowning at the goddess in white. "Tabitha, check again. You know we're not in last place."

She raises a perfect eyebrow at him. "You always came in first when I was your co-pilot."

She turns and flounces off. Cape flying in a way I wish I could pull off.

"*Okay*," I whisper.

Keston scrambles off the boat and ties up next to the jetty. He helps me out and then marches over to a man with a clipboard. "Hey, Oliver, has anyone else arrived yet?"

Oliver shakes his head. "You're the first boat back, Kes. As usual."

Keston turns a winning smile on me.

"We won, CJ," he grins.

I want to smile back and wave my hands in a victory salute, but the woman, Tabitha, is glaring at me.

It makes sense that Keston has exes on the island, but he's never talked about them. I'm not prepared for the darts of jealousy coursing from her eyes.

Keston gathers up our pirate booty from the boat and heads over to Oliver to check that we have everything on the list.

Oliver holds up the mermaid shell we retrieved from the bottom of Mermaid Pool.

"Yo, man, this is a perfect triton. You want to keep it?"

Keston glances at me.

I nod my head up and down. "Yes, please."

I already know where I'm putting it in his house. Right on

the kitchen counter to hold down the napkins that threaten to blow away every time a breeze sweeps through.

Before Oliver categorizes our bounty, other boats roar up to the dock.

Amidst a lot of laughing, teasing, and name-calling, they hurtle their booty off their boats and demand a recount.

"There's no way that a Yankee beat us," Starr chortles.

"See, you didn't win," says Tabitha, appearing by my side. She holds up a pristine, laminated paper.

"The Rules for this Pirate Regatta say that only residents can enter. It's to keep out the foreigners who come down in their fancy, fast boats."

To me, she says, "This is a local event. For St. Nicholas islanders. I'm afraid you're disqualified."

Keston walks over, bronzed skin still wet from our swim, dark tousled curls dropping water at my feet.

If "masculine" had a poster boy, he'd be it.

He peers at the "Rules."

Tabitha hands it to me. She points a gleaming, pink-tipped nail at Rule #1.

"Where did this come from? I've never seen it before in my life." Keston frowns at her.

"You did say there aren't any Rules," I chime in. Like I'm offering supporting testimony at a trial.

Tabitha narrows her eyes. "And you are?"

My heart beats weirdly out of sync—too fast for the problem at hand, which is to introduce myself.

"I'm . . . ."

Keston steps between me and Tabitha. "*My future wife.* Which makes her an islander, too."

"Wait, what?"

But he doesn't respond to me. Just takes the "Rules" out of my hand and passes it back to the vision in white.

His words "my future wife" resound inside me like a clanging bell.

The pack of soggy, drunken fishermen behind us burst into raucous applause.

"*Ooooh*, Loverboy is getting married," says Starr.

"Never thought I'd see the day," Captain Shaq agrees.

Another fisherman, called Beast, in a rasta-colored netted shirt revealing the same sleek muscles they all possess, apparently from hauling nets daily, dries his hands on his non-existent shirt and hands Keston a beer.

"Congratulations, pardner. Now we stand a chance with the other beauties."

Keston accepts the beer with a grin. "Thanks, Beast. I'm sure there is a Beauty just for you."

The air of good feelings is infectious. I find myself smiling at Beast and Starr, clicking my bottle of water with Shaq.

"I wanna sing at the wedding ceremony," declares a shiny bald man with a grizzled grey beard, clutching a bottle of 150-proof rum. His nickname is Redfish.

They all go by nicknames. I don't know any of their real names. And it appears Keston's nickname is '*Loverboy.*' How did I not realize that?

Redfish raises his rum bottle to use as a microphone. He sings at the top of his voice, "*Now that we found love.*"

The men join him, giving the oldie-but-goodie song a whole new vibe.

I never imagined it as my wedding song . . . or that my wedding song would be sung by a group of intoxicated fishermen.

Keston sips his beer, totally nonchalant about the fact that he's just "proposed" publicly.

Tabitha fans herself with the Rules, her pretty face in a scowl.

My alert monitor is Orange. There's some undercurrent going on that I don't quite understand.

"Hey, Oliver," Keston calls out. "Are we disqualified?"

Oliver scratches his thick grey hair. "It appears that you may be. Until you get married, that is."

Fishermen start booing at Oliver.

My sense of injustice summons anger at Tabitha, who created the Rules solely to get back at Keston—for something.

That old bottle of rum is important to him. He worked hard to finish his boat on time. Today, he excelled at getting to each destination and retrieving each item before everyone else.

"I have a suggestion," I speak up.

The fisherfolk dim down their exuberance a tad.

All eyes are on me.

"Yes?" Tabitha says with disdain. "What is it?"

"Can I see those Rules again?" I ask. Tabitha pauses before reluctantly handing me the list.

"Your rules say no foreigners with fast, fancy boats can enter. But I don't have a fancy boat. Or any boat at all. So, I don't count under Rule #1."

I don't mention that Keston has declared his boat "ours."

Everyone goes, "Oooohhhh."

I hold up a hand. "And . . . ."

The green of her eyes intensifies. Like a poisonous cloud descending on me.

"In the spirit of fairness, Keston and I will forfeit the prized rum if all the fishermen agree it is the right thing to do."

"What?" Keston stutters.

I place a hand on his arm.

Tabitha's eyes laser focus on my hand.

Meanwhile, the fishermen huddle together, talking over each other. Some curse. Some pull out cigarettes and light them. Puffing away in the thick of discussion.

After five minutes, Redfish says to Oliver, "Nah, man. Loverboy wins fair and square. He has the fastest boat. And his co-pilot ain't bad."

He winks at me.

"Thank you," I mouth back.

"Give Keston the rum," someone shouts. It's followed by a chorus of voices repeating those words.

Keston grins and kisses my hand. "You're a genius, CJ. How'd you know they'd say we won? After they've been trying to beat me for years."

I point at the swaying hips of the fishermen dancing to the reggae blaring from speakers as the Pirate Regatta party gets underway.

Women in cute party clothes hand out plates of rice and beans and stewed chicken.

The delicious scents waft my way. My stomach rumbles in response.

"I may not know St. Nicholas islanders well," I tell him. "But I recognize good guys when I see them."

I don't mention that I've been picking juries for years and that I've taken classes in reading people.

"Oh, yeah," he plucks my chin. "It could have gone the other way. I didn't take you for a gambling woman."

"What the heck do you think this trip is about? I'm gambling my entire life on you. On us."

He sobers up. "You are. Aren't you."

He wraps strong arms around my shoulders and hugs me close. "I love you, CJ. Thank you."

I'm pressed too close to his lovely pecs to speak without suckling one of his naughty-looking nipples.

"I'd say today was a win-win," he says. "Thanks to you."

"Team effort," I reply.

Chapter Seven

The restroom is eerily quiet after the noise outside on the dock.

It's only after wringing out my hair in the sink that I sense someone behind me.

Tabitha stares at me, a tiny smile on her lips.

"I wouldn't get so happy if I were you," she says ominously.

"Um . . . Tabitha. My name is Carmela. I don't know what history you and Keston had, but . . . ."

"Have," she interrupts.

"What?"

"We still *have* history. Women like you come and go. He always returns to me. We've been a couple since secondary school, and no one has changed that."

"Oh." I feel a knife twist in my stomach. She sounds so certain.

Her words, "Women like you," linger in the air.

As if reading my mind, she says, "*Tourists.*"

I flinch as if I've been slapped.

"You think St. Nicholas is beautiful. Just fun and games. Until reality sets in and you discover how difficult it is to live without your food delivery, your overnight packages. Then you go scurrying back up north. To your comfy homes and your Targets."

Whoa.

Has this woman read my mind for real?

Just this morning, I was wishing for a Target. That famous red dot store where I can buy everything from bras to books. Target is my biggest fantasy down here.

"Just don't hurt him. Again."

She flicks her hair over her shoulder and saunters out.

I'm left standing in a puddle of sink water, my denim shorts creased and my tee shirt damp. My hair is a wild, curly mess, and I have no makeup to hide behind.

But I can only think about her warning not to hurt Keston again.

What if he hurts me first? What if I give up my entire life for him, and he leaves me?

For the beautiful Tabitha.

A St. Nicholas islander. With whom he has a romantic history.

How come he never mentioned her?

Just when I was basking in the glow of Keston's words that one day we'd be married, the Universe cast a chill over my heart, with lingering fears about our future creeping in.

Chapter Eight

The Pirate Regatta party is spread out on the beach, with a million stars overhead. Food tables groan under coal pots filled with rice, peas, and stewed chicken that women brought from their homes.

There are bowls piled high with curry goat and crab. A giant pot of boiling water sits on a wood-burning fire.

Women wearing aprons covered in flour throw the dough into the boiling water to make dumplings as large as my hand.

The islanders use the thick white dumplings to scoop up their food and sauce. The dumplings are basically edible spoons.

A reggae band warms up on the sand. I don't know anyone so I'm relieved when Mrs. Harris from St. Nicholas Library and Historical Museum comes over and talks to me.

Keston introduced us during my first week back on the island. It feels like ages ago, even though it was only three weeks earlier.

I'd gone in to see if I could borrow books from the library and check out the museum.

The next thing I knew, I'd been drafted to help catalog boxes of documents and artifacts that had been dropped off months ago. I ended up going to the museum for several days to complete that task under Mrs. Harris's hawk eyes.

While I loved the experience, I found it strange that almost no one came to the library or museum. Not even school kids. Mrs. Harris said it was because everything is on the Internet now. And because of TikTok.

But the museum has loads of cool stuff. It's a real shame no one visits it, not even tourists.

"Carmela Jones. It's good to see you again."

"You too, Mrs. Harris."

"Thank you for your help at the museum. You're welcome to come back anytime. In fact, we will form a book club if you want to take part?"

"Me? I don't know anyone here."

She pats my arm. "Exactly. You can change that. Come by and get the list of names and phone numbers of those who'd be interested. You can call them and set it all up. Thursday evenings or Saturday afternoons would work for me."

This woman is a genius at delegating tasks. I could learn a thing or two from her.

She waves and walks off, a big smile on her face. "Mission accomplished," she's probably saying to herself.

"Why do I feel as if she's drafted me again but makes it seem as if I volunteered?"

Keston, who has sauntered up to my side after taking an actual shower in the fisherman's building, looks and smells fresh and delicious, unlike me, who took a sink splash.

"She's looking out for you. Trying to keep you from falling into my evil hands."

"Too late."

He plants a soft kiss on my hair as I relax into him. He's solid and strong. His six-foot-two frame would tower over most people back in the States. But here, he's just above average height.

Looking up through my eyelashes, I ask, "Why do the fishermen get real showers and the women's bathroom is bare bones?"

"It's to compensate for the dangerous job they do every day."

"Oh, okay, I can't complain about that."

"But you'll try to," he snickers, pinching my side.

I smack his arm away and stand up tall. "Let's get our food before it's all gone."

"*Someone* learned to eat in case of an emergency," he teases.

"Damn right."

When we first met, I picked at my food, skipped meals, and dieted a lot. Now, after being stranded on an island with Keston, I learned to stock up on my calories. With no shame. The more the better.

After filling our plates with delicious-smelling food, Keston guides me to a smooth log at the edge of the sea. The log looks washed clean from the rain and bleached by the sun.

It doesn't look like the softest of seats. Keston whips off his jersey and spreads it on the log for us to sit on.

"You don't have to do that," I say, while thinking, *thank God he did that.*

"Pretend you can't see me rolling my eyes," he teases.

This man knows me well.

I settle onto the log and sigh happily. "This is nice. Thank you."

We're close enough to hear the laughter and music. But far enough to feel as if we're in our own private world.

Shallow waves curl near our bare feet, leaving behind kisses of white foam on the sand.

"You did good out there, CJ. You can be my co-pilot anytime." Keston settles his plate on his lap and digs in with his oversized dumpling.

"Other than the fish thing," I mutter, trying to steer my food onto the dumpling. There must be an easier way to eat this.

"No one's perfect," he says.

I roll my eyes. His ex defies that notion. I bet she's not struggling to pick up her food.

"Do you need help there?" He eyes my clumsy attempt to scoop up food and sauce with my dough.

"I'm okay." I'm determined to try and fit in. I've not advanced very far at it in the past few weeks. Something the fishermen tease Keston about all the time.

They always ask him, "Has she learned to clean a fish yet?"

Apparently, that's one of the barometers for being a St. Nicholas islander. Whether I can gut and clean a fish, fillet it, and cook it up in a nice sauce.

To which I always shiver and say, "Never happening."

I kiss him on his cheek to distract him from my plate. How can I manage chopsticks but can't hold a flat dumpling between my thumb and forefinger? Seriously?

"You seem to be making some friends. I saw you talking to Mrs. Harris."

I break into a smile. "I like her. She said that since I helped her organize the boxes of documents, I could come back anytime. She's forming a book club."

Keston's eyes shine at me. "That's cool. You can read your romance books with them."

I scoff. "*Not*. Can you imagine the scandal if I handed them one of my steamy reads? I'd be kicked off the island."

"They *are* pornographic."

"They are not. They're hot."

He scratches his head. "I won't be jealous as long as your books don't grow a penis."

I laugh. "There's more than one way to wave your freak flag."

He smacks his forehead. "Don't steer our conversation in that direction, darling. Or else your back will be hitting this log. And your legs will be dancing on my shoulders. And trust me, I won't care if Mrs. Harris sees it instead of reads about it."

I push his shoulder. "You wouldn't dare."

"Wouldn't I?"

I eye him warily as I continue dipping my dumpling and sucking the sauce off the edge of it. The dipping and sucking is awakening a rush of excitement.

It's been a full day since Keston Kips aroused my body with his tongue. My poor pussy is having withdrawal symptoms.

Chapter Nine

After we've finished eating and washed our plates in the sea, reminding me of our days stranded together, we cuddle on the log.

Well, as much as a person can get comfortable sitting on a round hard piece of wood.

"You see Lucy?" I ask. His favorite star is the one made up

of trillions of diamonds which astronomers named Lucy after the Beatles song, *Lucy in the Sky with Diamonds.*

"I need a much stronger telescope for that," he says, resting his head on my lap and stretching out his legs.

The position triggers instant anxiety from the last time we sat like this. I bite my lip and push that horrific memory away.

"I still don't feel like part of St. Nicholas," I tell him. "Everyone's treating me so politely. Like I'm a guest. Except for the fishermen, that is. They're pranksters."

"People will treat you like a guest for a long time. You should enjoy it. Plus . . . ."

"What?"

He sits up and faces me. "It doesn't help that you live at the Cocoa Reef Resort. In one of the high-end villas. Nothing local about that."

"Where do you want me to live?" I huff.

"With me."

I crisscross my legs too fast. Sand flies into my eyes.

"Ouch!"

"You don't have to attack yourself."

"I didn't. My foot kicked up the sand by mistake. Are you mad I don't want to move in?" I ask.

"Not mad. More like disappointed."

"We've talked about this, Keston. I don't feel comfortable living with you so soon. In such close quarters. That doesn't mean I don't love you. Because I do."

His beach cottage, though cute, is a one-bedroom with a deck.

There's a lot of surrounding land and a pink coral sand beach in front, but still . . . where would I set up bookcases and a desk? Or have space to myself?

But I can't tell him this. It sounds petty.

"We just met," I say lamely.

I deserve the glare I get back.

"Fine," I grumble. "I'll consider it again."

He raises both hands like he's going to surrender. But then drops them and sighs.

"I love you woman. I want to wake up next to you every day. Go to sleep next to you every night. I want you near me."

"Clingy much?" I tease him, making a pouty face to reflect his own.

He grabs my arms and pins them around his neck. His lips find mine.

Forget that we just ate chicken and dumplings, his kisses are hungry.

I feel myself falling into the magic of his tongue caressing my mouth. The tingle of his hands running up and down my sides and legs, my back, all over like he's tracing every line and curve of my body to remember forever. Knowing him, that's exactly what he's doing.

I'm so relaxed from his kiss that I almost tumble off the log.

Keston's arms steady me.

When we raise our heads, I hear clapping. At first, I believe they're clapping for our blatant PDA. But the applause is for *The Mangoes,* the reggae band.

"We're missing the concert," I say.

He uncrosses my legs and pulls me toward him. Wraps my legs around his waist instead.

"Dude, I want to make a good impression."

"Too late for that, woman."

Part of me loves his playful show of affection. Another part feels like we're being reckless with our future. Suppose we don't work out. Suppose it turns out I can't live on this tiny island. Suppose Keston gets sick of me. How do we recover from such overt displays of love and affection? We'd be laughing stocks.

Keston lifts my chin. Stares into my eyes.

"I *am* clingy. I *am* needy. I am addicted to *you*." He inhales my hair and neck. Like a bear sniffing his next meal.

"Oh God, haven't you heard about *codependence*?" I smack his chest. "It's not a good thing."

He shakes his head. "Never heard of that. How could loving you and wanting to be with you be a bad thing? It must be a first-world problem, as you guys say. If you don't like it, sue me. Another thing you say up there."

"I can actually sue you, too, you know."

"Fine," he presses his lips against mine. "I plead guilty."

He moves even closer if that's possible. Raises up my hips and yanks me tighter against his open legs. We're as close as we can get without him being inside me.

"That's not how the law works. You must be arrested first."

"Give me a few minutes. I might be."

I feel what he's silently promising. His tire iron of a cock presses against my soft pussy in sweet anguish.

"Your cock has a mind of its own."

"So does your pussy."

"I can't argue with that."

"But you'll try."

I smack him again. "I hate how well you know me."

"I hate that you won't let me know you more."

"In time.

"Time is for thieves."

"What?"

He grins against my lips. "I'm going to steal time to keep you here longer. Forever."

The sweetness of his kiss is something I could never forget.

"Maybe you won't have to steal it. Maybe I'll stay."

Chapter Ten

I already know how tonight will end. With steamy sex on cool sheets. My cries of bliss will echo across the sea.

"Not here," I whisper desperately as his massive steel pushes up against my well of desire.

He nibbles my ear. "We could go in the water."

"At night? With all the big fish swimming about? No way."

He pouts, as cute as if he were five. "Scaredy cat."

"I cross my arms. Mostly to stop me from dragging him off behind a coconut tree and yanking down his pants.

Or to lay down in the cool sand and feel his tongue deep diving into my honey pot.

That magic tongue would slide its way between my folds, lick my slit, circle around my pulsating clit, then plunge mercilessly in and out of my pussy until there's nothing but sweet, sweet oblivion.

His tongue can make me come in less than five minutes. We could literally go into the dark trees, and he could bring me to a frenzy before anyone missed us.

As if aware that I'm seriously considering it, one of his callused fingers slides between my shorts and strokes my pussy.

A jolt of excitement thrills through me.

His other arm wraps around pulling my head to his shoulder.

"There're people all over the beach," I argue weakly.

"Everyone's dancing," he says soothingly. "Relax. It'll feel so good," he whispers like a bad devil on my shoulder.

His finger works itself beneath the flimsy cloth of my panties.

"Oh baby," he breathes. "You're wet."

"I know." My voice is husky and breathless.

I can't speak. Sparks are flying through me. My body tenses on the edge of falling off a cliff.

He presses his finger to the entrance of my pussy. His fingertip circles around it like a butterfly kissing the lips, the labia, then finally . . . glides into the deep deep center of me. Rubbing my G-spot with careful control.

My flower widens beneath his attention. I want to spread

my legs so bad. Push his head between my legs. Feel his tongue and fingers at the same time.

I whimper, "Don't stop."

"Never," he growls.

As if knowing we're on a deadline, my pussy ramps up its wetness. Juices flow like a river.

"You're soaking baby. God, this is agony. I want to fuck you so bad. Lean you back on this log and take you right here."

My voice is a whimper. I want to beg him to take me. Drag me to a dark spot and fuck me from behind. From on top. Fuck me every way he can until I can't take it anymore.

"I'm going to come," I cry.

"Come for me, baby." His voice is soft but fierce. Demanding. "I want you to pour out on my hand. Give me all of you."

His thick thumb presses down on my clit, releases pressure, and presses again. His long dexterous fingers stroke, caress, slide into my pussy, rubbing the G-zone I didn't know I had before I met him.

The frenzy is coming. I shut my eyes. The pressure builds like a roller coaster climbing up a hill. Slowly. Surely. Cresting.

Holy moly. This is going to be a rocking orgasm. The kind that shakes the trees.

His fingers ramp up their action. They rub faster. Pluck my clit firmer. Plunge through my juices with abandon.

And then. Whoosh! I'm flying into the night.

Every nerve ending in my sweet clit explodes. Flashes of light follow behind my eyeballs.

Everything ceases to exist except Keston Kips and my pussy.

A scream rises in my throat, but Keston's mouth closes on mine. He catches my scream. Takes my breath away literally.

His fingers do not falter. They keep up the constant pressure and the same movement, never missing a beat.

My poor, sweet pussy weeps with gratitude.

Coming back to reality, my eyes pop open.

At that moment I see Tabitha's glare stabbing me with icicles all the way from across the beach. She must know what he's doing to me.

I don't know whether to feel embarrassed. Or relieved.

Chapter Eleven

Keston and I rejoin the pirate party. I'm avoiding Tabitha's missile-seeking eyes at all costs.

The band's short break is over. The lead singer says in a deep, sexy voice, "Good evening, mateys. My name is Carlos Campbell, and we are *The Mangoes*. You can catch us every Friday and Saturday night at the *Shipwreck Tavern.*"

"*The Mangoes*? Such a cute name," I chuckle.

Keston's lips slide into a smirk. "As cute as the *Cranberries*?"

I choke on my comeback.

"Or as cute as the *Black Eyed Peas*." He ticks off his fingers. "Or *Bread*? Not to mention, *Cream*. Who names their band, *Cream*?"

I'm not sure if it's the rum punch's fault that I find Keston's defense of *The Mangoes* so funny, but I'm almost falling over with the giggles.

When I finally control myself, I gasp, "You forgot the *Smashing Pumpkins*."

"There's no such group," Kes snorts.

"Uh huh."

He tickles me and I burst out laughing again.

"There is," I swear.

"What are some of their songs?"

I rack my brain. "I don't know any off the top of my head. But I'm not making it up. Can I help it if *your* musical knowledge is lacking?"

Keston's white-toothed grin lights up his face. "That's why I love you."

"Why?" I sober up.

"You're not afraid to hurt my feelings."

"Oh, you're just now figuring that out?"

He grimaces. "Maybe I'm a sucker for pain. But I don't have to wonder what you're thinking. It's the secret of our relationship. You always let me know."

Nuh uh. Right now, I'm burying my feelings of unease about you and Tabitha's past.

I don't say that aloud though. I leave the skepticism and doubt to hover in midair like twin boomerangs ready to swing back my way when I least expect them.

"I always heard the secret to a strong relationship is compromise," I speak confidently, relaying the wisdom I learned from my girlfriends.

He lets out a loud, "*Bahahaha.*"

"What's so funny?" My hands curl into fists, ready to rumble.

"You compromise?" He shakes his head. "Does that concept exist in your CJ world?"

I swat his arm. Sometimes I can't tell if he's joking. Or hiding truths with humor.

Another reason not to live together yet. Suppose he isn't joking. And this is all a set-up for a huge letdown.

Like what happened with Marcus. After five long years of dating a man I believed would want to marry and start a family, only to find out he had no such intention.

Imagine going through that again at my age?

Forty is the new thirty in every way but one. And honestly, I'm ready to get married to a man I love. Ready to have children. And a dog and a cat and . . . maybe, even learn to compromise.

"Earth to CJ." Keston waves a hand in front of my face.

"What?" I snarl. Why'd he ruin my beautiful fantasy? I was just about to bake a dream pie or two.

"What can I do for you?" I huff.

"Woman, stop stressing about whether you can learn to compromise. I was joking. With a capital J."

I step back to gaze into his eyes. "How do you know what I was thinking about?"

He rolls his eyes. "You, my dear, live in here." He pats his heart. "The good, the bad, and the . . . ."

"Don't you dare say, '*ugly!*'"

He shrugs. "The point is, I can tell when you're struggling. I'm here for you. Through everything."

I can't help it, I giggle.

Luckily for us, *The Mangoes* begin to croon Bob Marley's ode to love.

Everyone on the beach, including me and Kes, sings along to *One Love*. The song you'll hear all over the world, in airports, bars and restaurants, on beaches, in cities, and on ferries and trains, from Jamaica to Japan.

If a reggae song can bring together people from all over the globe, what else can do that?

I glance up at the handsome man next to me. My love. My annoying ride-or-die. Is there a secret I don't know about that can glue us together?

As we lift our voices in song, the fishermen raise their lighters to the sky. I sway side to side, standing between Keston's wide-legged stance.

With the stars aglow above me, a soft shifting carpet of sand beneath my feet, and Keston's arms wound around my waist, I feel the happiest I've ever been in my life.

This must mean I belong here, right?

Chapter Twelve

Later, after the food is put away and the children are asleep wrapped in towels and big tee shirts, families crank up their cars and head home.

The band plays on as fishermen dance with their girlfriends. Some people sit on the sand in groups chatting and laughing. Keston and I find a place on the outskirts of one group.

A bottle of dark rum is being passed around. Most pour a capful of rum into their cups of pineapple juice.

I decline and pass the bottle to Keston. I've had enough rum punches for the night.

"This could be a movie," I yawn, leaning my head on his chest as we sit on the sand.

Someone has built a fire from coconut husks. It sends orange flames shooting into the sky.

Keston and I hold on tightly to each other.

"The only person who didn't dance tonight is Tabitha," I remark, oh so casually. "Although many asked her. She seemed to be staring at us."

"I didn't notice."

How could he not notice her stalkerish vibe?

"What's up with you and her?" I ask turning around to face him.

I can't help myself. You can promise not to do something or say something all night long. Then wham. It slips out in a mush of anxiety vomit.

He ties a clean bandana around his curls.

Is he stalling?

He clears his throat.

He is.

Finally, he speaks, searching for words. Almost as if what he has to say is going to be painful. But to whom?

I brace myself.

"She came to the hospital every day when I was recovering from my leg surgeries. She was a real friend."

"Every day?" That's a surprise. I only came once. Then I left him.

He nods. "I told her about you. She knows how I feel. What Tabitha and I had was in the past."

Yeah, but does Tabitha know that?

I'm dying to ask how far back in the past they dated, but I'm holding my tongue. He'll tell me if it's important. I must believe in our relationship for it to grow. Easier said than done.

Telling myself it's normal for Keston to have an ex, and coming face to face with said ex who exudes a possessive vibe are two different things.

"She said you wouldn't return to St. Nicholas," he continues, his eyes far away like he's still in that hospital bed.

"Really?"

His head drops. A rare thing for him. "I believed her."

Raw pain muddles his voice. My heart clutches tightly into a ball. I shouldn't have pushed him. What a monster I am. Forcing him to recall an extremely painful time of his life. When he almost lost his leg.

"I'm sorry." I rub his arm. "We don't have to talk about this."

"It was so hard," he whispers. "When you left."

"I didn't want to leave you. But you told me to go." I stare at him, willing him to understand how hard it was for me too.

We never discussed the first and last time we saw each other after our rescue. But it's part of our foundation. How long can we ignore it?

I remember the sharp pain I felt when he told me to leave St. Nicholas. That he could not give me what I needed. That rejection sits like a wolf at my door. Ready to blow all that we're building apart.

I understand why he did it in theory, but the hurt I felt was larger than life itself. It sucked me into a depression.

"You went through a lot when we were stuck on No Man's Land." He shudders as if remembering the horrible parts. "I didn't think you needed to go through more. Plus, let's not forget your ex-boyfriend demanded that I never talk to you again."

Right. Marcus and Tabitha would make a great pair.

He sighs. "The worst experience of my life was watching you walk out that door. Leg pain came and went. There were pills for that. My heart never stopped hurting."

"Well, I'm here now." I paste on my best optimistic smile. Which is a stretch for me. I'm a glass needs more kinda gal.

He kisses my lips and leans back. "That's to seal our past with our future. You and me, baby. We are one love. Just like the legend sang."

My hand caresses his handsome face. "Yes, one love forever."

"I hope nothing comes between us." I'm thinking of Tabitha. Of my life in New York. Of not fitting in here on St. Nicholas. All things that could potentially tear us apart.

"Nothing will come between us, CJ. I promise you that. Now kiss me, woman."

After a deep kiss that shoots stars to the back of my eyeballs, Keston says, "Bet you didn't know I was coming to get you. If you didn't return here, I was coming to New York City. One way or another."

He'd mentioned that before. His plan was to come north and kidnap me.

I grab his hands. "New York is the last place I'd expect to see you. You'd be like Crocodile Dundee up there. So out of place with your machete."

"I love that movie. My mom had it on DVD and I watched it every day."

"Well, I'm glad we didn't have to act out that film."

"*I'm* glad you're right where you belong." He squeezes me close. Rests his head on top of my hair. I feel his words more than I hear them.

"Every day I laid in that hospital bed, I thought about what you were doing. I wondered if you were thinking about me. Whether you missed our tiki hut and our waterfall. Most of all I hoped you were okay. Tabitha showed me social media posts about you and Marcus at events."

Of course, she did.

"I hoped you were happy."

Tears form in my eyes. This man touches the deepest parts of my soul with his heartfelt words.

"I missed you. I just didn't see how we could have a future together," I admit.

"And now?" He leans back to catch my chin with one hand. "What do you think now?"

I stifle the urge to barnacle my flighty self to his solid anchor.

"The jury is still out," I say lightly.

Dark shadows cover the usual glee in his eyes.

"I understand that St. Nicholas can't compare with New York. But I'm going to do whatever it takes to make sure you're happy here," he says. "You still have three weeks of your sabbatical from work. I hope to change your mind about going back. I don't think I can survive you leaving me a second time."

His words catch me off guard. We have not discussed what will happen when my leave from work is up. I took six weeks off and we've already used up three of them, mostly in his bed.

"I'm happy with *you*," I speak truthfully.

"But . . . ."

"I feel like such an outsider. Everyone here is either related or going to be."

He chuckles. "True."

"Then there's that awful donkey tramping through your yard who insists on stealing my clothes. Your fishermen friends make me the brunt of their jokes. And let's not forget about Tabitha. She scares the hell out of me."

He throws back his head and laughs. Which gives me immense relief.

All this talk about leaving each other is causing me anxiety.

"We'll find a way for you to feel like one of us. No one can wave a magic wand and connect with everyone."

"Except Bob Marley."

"There's only one legend," he agrees.

"What do the St. Nicholas islanders love as much as they love reggae?"

Keston snorts. "The only thing we love as much as reggae is our rum."

I laugh. "I'll need to plan something that involves rum, then."

His forehead puckers in deep concentration. "Carmela Jones, CJ, honeypot, all I ask is that you move in as soon as possible. I hate knowing you're on this island and not in my bed."

"Grumpy much?"

"No. Horny much is more like it."

I snuggle up to him. "I knew you only wanted me for my body."

"Damn right."

Chapter Thirteen

"You did it again, bruh." It's Captain Shaq, congratulating Keston on his win.

"Nice going, Speed Racer," says an older gentleman in a dashiki.

"When are you going to give the youngsters a break?" asks a

guy who's about twenty. "You have enough of those prized bottles of rum."

Keston promises to share his rum.

"We're dipping out. You need a ride, man?" one of his friends asks.

Keston looks at me. "Not faster than driving the boat back, but drier."

The harbor is full of boats tied up, some to the jetty, some on buoys, and others are pulled onto the sand. It seems everyone is driving home tonight and leaving their boats here.

I waded in to get to shore, and I don't want to wade back out now that I'm nice and dry. And slightly dizzy with rum punch.

"Oh, absolutely," I smile. "We'll take a ride."

We follow Keston's friend, Alex, to a car that looks like it should be in the *Fast & Furious* franchise.

In the back seat of the heavily tinted car, I push all thoughts of Tabitha St. Clair from my mind and collapse next to Keston. It's been a long day and night.

He pulls me gently into the circle of his arms. I feel myself nodding off as the men discuss a celebrity golf tournament. It will be held at Cocoa Reef Resort at Christmas in a few months.

"How much is the prize?" Keston asks excitedly. "I want in."

My eyes are closing, but they pop open again, "You play golf?"

"Don't sound so surprised. I'm insulted."

"Kes is the top golfer for *The Rasta Blasters*," chirps Alex. "That's his four-person team."

"Wait a minute, how come I didn't know you played golf?"

"It's been difficult to play since the accident." He stretches out his leg in the back seat of the car. "But if I'm going to win that tournament. I need to step up my game."

"Prize is 10 Gs I heard," Alex says. "And you're *always* on your game, pal."

Keston whistles through his teeth. "Ten thousand American dollars?"

"Yup."

Kes stares out the window.

What's he thinking about?

"Let me know if I can help," I murmur.

His lips graze my forehead. "Of course, baby."

Alex looks at us through the rear-view mirror. "You gotta come back for the tournament, CJ."

They're innocent words. But they trigger a feeling of sadness.

Everyone must think I'm leaving soon. As if what Keston and I have is just a vacation fling. Tabitha hopes so.

Keston must understand how I'm feeling because he says loudly, "She's not leaving. So, she doesn't have to *come back*."

Alex smacks his steering wheel. "You don't have to convince me, man. I hope you guys work out."

"We will," says Keston. "We survived No Man's Land together."

Alex taps the steering wheel. In a voice that is not at all sarcastic, he says to me, "Keston accomplishes whatever he goes after. It's his superpower."

"What is?" I ask.

At the same time, Keston groans. "Please, I don't have a superpower."

"No, let me tell her," Alex interjects.

"I'm all ears," I tell Alex.

To Keston, I whisper, "My baby has superpowers?"

Alex starts talking as we travel down the dark, empty roads.

"Back in school, Keston would surprise everyone by signing up for stuff nobody wanted to do. Like when our school was putting on *King Lear*, he played King Lear. Nobody wanted to memorize all that old English language. But he did it. Easily. The play went on to win in a Caribbean-wide contest.

"Then, our football captain got sick. Soccer, you call it. Anyway, Kes stepped in, and they won! Went on to play in the whole damn Caribbean league. Our school has a case full of Keston Kip's trophies. In golf, tennis, soccer, drama, and even art. You name it. He can do it. People say it's because of what's in his jeans."

"Man, stop talking your nonsense," Keston barks.

"In his jeans?" I ask, confused.

How does everyone know about his masterpiece of a cock?

"Not his jean pants," Alex chuckles. "His genes like his chromosomes."

"Oh," I laugh weakly, still a little tipsy.

"Get your mind out of the gutter," Keston whispers. "We're almost home."

I smack his wrist. "Says the man with no restraint on a beach full of people."

"I didn't hear any complaints," he snickers.

Alex turns off the main road and heads down the dirt track to Keston's house.

"Kes, I have to tell her the best part."

"Yes. You do. Please enlighten me." I smirk at Keston. "I want to know what's in this man's *genes*."

My hand pats the lump of steel in his pants. He grabs my hand and presses it down harder. I gulp. Who's winning this battle here?

"It's got nothing to do with my genes," Keston says exasperatedly. "I just practice a lot. Which none of your lazy high school asses wanted to do."

The car hits a big pothole.

Alex curses and focuses on the rough terrain.

"Dude, get your road fixed."

"I like it this way. Nobody bothers me."

"Are you going to tell me the best part?" I interrupt their banter. "About Keston's genes?"

Alex snorts. "He can tell you. It's no secret."

I look pointedly at Keston. "Tell me."

When he doesn't say a word, Alex blurts, "He's the great-great-great — I'm not sure how many greats — grandson of an African prince turned pirate king and a Scottish princess from Great Britain."

"Wait, what?"

I don't think my eyes can open any wider as I turn them on the man by my side.

"You are African and European royalty?"

"Technically, Scottish," he says. "And no, it's a myth. Stop telling stories, dude."

"It isn't a myth, and you know it. You are the descendant of their sole child. It wasn't exactly a celebrated union. Black pirate, white princess." Alex laughs. "And the Internet thinks it has scandals today. Just imagine back then."

"Wow! This is almost too incredible to believe."

"Which is why it isn't true," Keston says. "There's never been any DNA proof. It's all speculation."

"Yet, it's a story the entire island knows." Alex circles his lowrider, dark-tinted car in the yard and pulls up next to Keston's beach house. He turns toward me. "Ask anyone."

"Is that why you own all this beachfront property?" I gesture out the window at the immense stretch of land and beach, trees, and river.

Alex laughs. "Yup. All part of the mystery of Keston Kips' heritage."

I clamber out of the back of the car like I'm climbing out of a cave. Keston takes my hand to help me out.

"Don't ever get a lowrider," I mutter under my breath.

"Thanks for the ride, my man," Keston slaps the car's hood.

"And the history lesson," I call out.

A loud hee-hawing comes from the woods near the clothesline. But the donkey is not what's on my mind right now.

"How come you never told me all this?"

"Maybe I want you to love me for who I am. A plain old bartender."

"Ha!" I scoff. "Mixing drinks is what you love doing. It's not *who* you are."

"Who am I, CJ.?"

I stare at the sky glittering with stars. "You are the man who sees more than most, feels more than most, and I love more than most."

A soft silence fills the air. I don't talk like this. Will he think I'm being sarcastic?

He sits on the bottom step and stretches out his injured leg.

It's healed now, but I cannot forget how it looked that night in the hurricane, broken and twisted when I thought we would both die. That image is on a loop playing in the back of my mind.

"That's why I love you so much," he says. "You make me feel as if I'm your hero."

I put one hand on a hip and tap my foot. "Keston Kips, you *are* my hero."

His eyes are stark and probing, his carefree happiness clouded by something I don't understand.

"I hope I will always be," he whispers.

I've never met anyone like Keston Kips. From day one on that hill by Cocoa Reef Resort when he was star gazing and mistook me for a fallen star because of my glittery dress.

How cute is that?

Macho and masculine but also loving and supportive. Happy and carefree. But also fully committed.

And not just to me. To everything in his life. His job as the supreme mixologist at the resort.

His fishermen friends, who he helps by pulling in their nets with them most evenings. Taking only a fresh fish as a thank you.

And his physical therapy which he pursues like a demon to be 100% again.

The question playing on my mind is, "Who or what am I committed to?"

Sitting on the deck after we showered properly and changed into soft pajamas (well, I put on soft pajamas, he put on an old pair of soccer shorts), feet tucked under me, gazing at the bazillion stars dotting the sky while Keston peers into his old telescope, I must say I'm committed to my mom, whom I'm closer to than ever before.

And my girlfriends, for always having my back for the past twenty years.

Also, even though I have not met her yet, other than the day she was born, I'm committed to my daughter, Lucy. She's coming to upstate New York to meet me and her grandmother at Thanksgiving. My heart thrills when I think about it. Only one more month.

And, of course, Keston. I am committed to him—heart, soul, everything.

But am I committed to living on St. Nicholas?

Can two people from completely different cultures and backgrounds make it work?

Like how an African prince turned pirate connected with a princess from Great Britain! I would love to hear that story.

Later, when Keston's warm body wraps itself around mine

and spoons me close for the entire night, I know I've never felt safer.

And all the pesky questions about whether we can make it work disappear.

The next morning, I awake to find Keston gone. The a/c blasts cool air. The sun beams through the curtains, making lacy patterns on the floor. His side of the bed is cool enough for me to realize he's been gone for a while.

He left a note.

He went to help the Pirate Regatta events committee clean up and bring his boat back. He added:

Help yourself to anything. I'll be back as soon as I can.

If you're bored you can redecorate the house to your liking.

So you can move in! ASAP.

I love you.

KK

I grin. Redecorate? He's joking. What would I fix? I wouldn't change a thing. Keston's home feels warm and lovely, with all the practical items he made himself.

Bamboo chairs on the porch, coconut-scented candles for when there's a power outage, and a pink conch shell as a door stopper.

Not to mention the placemats and coasters woven from palm branches.

Calabash shells are polished until they gleam and used as bowls, bird feeders, and soap holders in the outdoor shower.

It's perfect.

A braying comes from the yard. I peek out to see the donkey doing a high-stepping dance by the clothesline.

Is she nibbling on my jeans? No way!

"Go away!" I shout, walking down the front steps. But not too loudly, as I don't want her to stampede me or anything.

I know what Keston needs to add to his home. A clothes dryer! So the donkey will stop stealing my clothes from the line. I watch as she trots down the dirt road. Back to wherever she came from.

For one infinitesimal second, I miss having her grey and white loopy presence in the yard. Now that she's gone, everything feels too quiet.

Other than the sounds of the waves, the screeching parrots flying overhead, and oh yeah, the bamboo wind chimes. Nature is not quiet *at all*.

Chapter Fifteen

Back on the wooden deck, sunblock on my face and underwear on my butt, I sip lemongrass tea and assess my options.

I could call for a taxi to pick me up and drive me back to the resort. Having a free villa at the Cocoa Reef Resort for six weeks (to make up for them leaving me on No Man's Land) is a blessing. I love having my own space.

But this is my first time alone at Keston's home. I should try to see how it feels to live here full-time. And not have a gorgeous, fully carpeted, luxury villa to run back to.

If this were my home for real, the first thing I'd do is call my friends and discuss what I learned about Keston last night. His ex may still be in love with him. And I'm dating a possible descendant of double royalty.

That second one sounds unreal. However, given the Caribbean islands' history during the last four hundred years, it is possible.

Giselle answers immediately.

"Feeling a bit lonely in paradise?" she jokes.

"No. That's why I have you. But I did learn some interesting information about Keston."

"Oh, do tell," says Giselle. "But let me get the rest of the gang on the call first."

Katana appears looking crazy-eyed. "What's going on?" she asks, scrubbing her face with her fists.

"You look wonderful," I say warmly. "Is the baby sleeping through the night yet?"

She snorts. "I thought you were calling to invite me on a vacay in the Caribbean with you."

I perk up. "You can come anytime. All of you."

Lisa, the astrophysicist who just got married, smiles into the video call. "Wow, CJ, you look so robust."

"Robust?" I squeak. "Do you mean I gained weight? Or as they say down here, 'put on size?'"

Lisa laughs. "No. I mean, you look fresh and healthy."

"Oh. Thank you. I feel great."

I remember Tabitha. "Except I think Keston's ex-girlfriend

wants him back and wants me off this island. Not necessarily in that order."

"This better be good. It's not even noon," Mikah joins the call, yawning her pretty face off. She's a freelance model who travels the world.

"It is," says Giselle. "CJ is dealing with ex-girlfriend issues."

'Well, it's not an issue yet." I fill them in on the bathroom scene where Tabitha told me I'd go running back home to shop.

"Harsh," Mikah mutters. "You need backup, CJ? Just let me know."

"I miss you guys. When are you all coming to visit me?"

"When we're invited to the wedding," Lisa says blandly.

"You have weddings on the brain, Mrs. Newlywed." I tease.

"It's one thing for her to be interested in him. Is Keston interested in her? That's the only thing that matters," Lisa says.

"It's a small island. They're friendly."

All my friends seem to mull over that.

"What does your gut say?" asks Katana.

I close my eyes and breathe deeply. "It says I'm out of my element. She's drop-dead gorgeous."

"You're no slouch," Mikah chirps, "and I should know."

"Thanks?"

"Let's get to more important topics," Mikah says. "Have you met *my* Mr. Right yet?"

Everyone laughs. Katana rolls her eyes.

"Maybe. There are some hunks down here. All taller than you."

"Oh yeah?" she says. "What about nice and kind and able to satisfy me in ways I've never known before?"

"That too," I say slyly. "If my man is anything to go by."

"Not like you need help meeting anyone," Katana adds snidely. "With all dem sugar daddies you're collecting."

Mikah snorts, "Don't hate. When I find the perfect man like you have, I'll settle down."

"Speaking of perfect men, is Keston still fine as sugar and hot like pepper?" Katana asks.

Memories of last night on the beach make me turn red. "Kind of."

They hoot and holler. I can't stop grinning.

"Then you have nothing to worry about from his ex-girlfriend," says Lisa. "It's like when Giselle was dating the football star in college. He had a ton of exes."

Giselle snaps her fingers. "This is not about me! For the record, he couldn't be trusted. But Keston can be, right?"

"Yes," I say with conviction in my heart.

"Remember, you can't control anyone's actions, like his exes; you can only control yours. So, don't react to her shenanigans." Lisa points out a strategy that has served us all well.

I sit back on the porch swing, legs stretched out, feet resting on the railing. The sun plays tic-tac-toe across my legs.

"Thanks for the reminder. Now, wait until you hear this."

My best friends give me their full attention. Even Katana and she has two babies.

I relay the story Alex told me in the car.

Dead silence.

"You guys still there?" I wave my hand in front of the phone screen. WiFi is spotty out by Keston's.

Giselle, a middle school principal, is the first to speak. "Is there any documentary proof of any of this?"

"Forget proof. I believe it," shouts Mikah. "This is the kind of history that's been buried for generations."

Katana nods in agreement, which almost never happens between her and Mikah. "But how unfair is it that first you're dating a hot billionaire, and now, you're getting your groove on with a prince?"

Lisa hoots. "CJ is a special woman."

"I am?"

"Yes, look at what you did on No Man's Land. Your feats went viral."

I frown. "That was life and death. But seriously, do you guys think it could be true?"

They're all nodding.

"Absolutely," says Katana. "You saw Bridgerton? This has got Shonda Rhimes all over it. She'd turn Keston's story into a Netflix drama everyone would watch."

We groan. She's been rewatching all the episodes and talking about them as if we didn't watch them together.

"At least it makes sense why he owns all that beachfront property," Lisa says. "He inherited it from a pirate."

"Or a princess," says Mikah.

"Women didn't own property back then, so probably the pirate," Giselle cuts in. "Can you give us the panoramic tour again, please? We must live through you."

I screw up my eyes. "You guys are kidding, right? You've seen his place a dozen times."

I turn the phone and make a sweep of the beach and rainforest.

"If this land once belonged to a pirate king and/or his British/Scottish princess, it must be worth . . . who knows!"

"Millions is my guess," says Mikah. "People would pay for the story alone."

"But Keston has no interest in selling any of it. So, its worth is in historical significance only."

I lapse into silence, recalling a conversation with Keston on my first day or two here. I'd asked him if all this land was his.

"For over two hundred years, this land has been Kipson land," he said.

"Kipson?"

"That was our name. One of my ancestors shortened it to Kips."

I didn't think any more about it.

"My goodness, CJ, it's gorgeous. And you get to live there." Katana sighs.

"I bet the view of the night sky is stunning." Lisa leans close to the phone. "It is, isn't it?"

"It is," I assure her. "We have an old telescope and watch the constellations at night. One of his many hobbies."

"Giving you crazy orgasms better be another," says Katana.

"No wonder you get pregnant so often," Mikah says sternly. "You can't keep it in your pants."

Katana sucks her teeth.

"We're getting off-topic ladies," says Giselle. "What's the name of the beach? Maybe I can look it up and see if it was connected to any pirate history. Check on Mr. Kips' heritage."

"Arawak Bay. Named after the first people who lived on the island. But I'm not investigating him."

"Well, you should." Giselle sounds exasperated. "Isn't that why you're there? To find out everything and decide whether to uproot your entire life?"

"Not *everything*. Besides, he's well-loved here. There's nothing to investigate."

"Let us decide that for you. Now, what do you know?" Mikah asks.

"I didn't mean to turn this into a probe. I was sharing the tale of him possibly being a descendant of an African prince slash pirate king for fun."

"So, you don't want to know about the ancestors of your future children? Whether they have pirate genes or royal blood, or both?"

I perk up. "I never thought of . . . *children*. Isn't that jumping ahead?"

Giselle clears her throat. "When you left on this six-week journey back to St. Nicholas to see if you and Keston Kips were meant to be, you promised to learn as much as you could to make a good decision."

"I know!" I cry. "It sounded so romantic when I was in New York. But now . . . ." I turn the camera around to show them the cottage.

"I'll be living in a tiny house with a man I met six months ago. I knew him for one week under stressful circumstances and didn't see him again until two weeks ago. It's scary."

"But you *lurve* each other," Lisa stresses. "True love triumphs."

"We do love each other," I agree.

"Why bother moving to St. Nicholas if you aren't considering marrying him?" Giselle asks. "And having the babies you long for?"

Giselle has a point.

"Be careful what you wish for," Katana says darkly. "That cute Barbie doll figure you have, CJ? Poof!" she snaps her fingers loudly.

"Don't listen to Katana," Lisa says. "Sometimes you must take a leap of faith. Forget about his past. Pirate or prince, doesn't matter."

"You sound like Keston. He says the past is the past. The future will take care of itself. And now is what we have."

"Wise man. We're specks in the cosmos. Enjoy your life now."

"Yes, Mrs. Astrophysicist," I laugh. "I'll try to do that."

"Anyway," Katana interjects. "If it's true, you could build a castle on the beach. To acknowledge his roots."

"No, Katana, I'm not building a castle on the beach."

Although. It's not the *worst* idea.

Chapter Sixteen

"Honey! I'm home."

The sound of Keston's rich baritone catapults my heart almost out of my chest. A big smile I don't intend lifts the corners of my mouth.

Damn! I want to be cranky.

I want to complain that he left me here for too long.

But he leaps up the front steps, grabs me up in his arms, and swings me around. His cheerfulness conquers my grumpiness and I'm a grinning ball of dandelion fluff.

I cross my arms on my chest when he puts me down. "I'm mad."

"Then let me make you feel better."

Before I can protest, he turns me around, leans me over the deck railing, props a cushion under my stomach, and yanks down my panties.

"Wait, what?"

I watch as my panties go flying across the porch. "I don't know why you bother to wear these things," he mutters. "They just get in the way."

"You can't make up for everything with sex."

But it's too late. My head is hanging over the flower beds. My hands grip the railing for balance. And his hot, wet tongue slides deep into the heat of my core.

His lips purr against my sensitive parts. "You don't like, baby? Say the word. I'll stop."

I grunt. A thickness I know well presses against my pussy.

"Are you fucking or sucking me, make up your mind?" I quarrel.

He laughs merrily. "Both. God, I missed you."

"It's only been four hours," I snap. I won't admit I've missed him too. He's wearing me down. Turning me into mush.

"You taste sweet like honey."

My smile returns. I can already feel the excitement building. It doesn't take long with this man. He stands up and I feel his thick heavy manhood entering my wet pussy.

"Yes, baby." He slides his cock in and out slowly. Bending forward to cup my breast. "I love this baby."

As soon as I think he's got the stroking part down, he pulls out.

"What the hell?"

But his tongue plunges into my pussy. Takes up where his cock left off. Swirling, stroking my pussy with a loud smacking noise.

Sure hard fingers circle my dark hole. Nerve endings twinge with excitement.

My legs shake.

"I'm going to come," I cry.

"Not yet."

He pulls his tongue away and I cry out. "No."

His cock plunges back into my pussy. It's torture. He pumps a couple times then pulls out, pressing his hot tongue where his cock abandoned.

This time I reach behind to grip his head. I hold his head to my ass, forcing him to lick my pussy.

"Oh God, right there," I murmur. "I can't bear it."

His mouth envelops my entire pussy. Tongue skating up and down like he's playing scales on a piano. My clit trembles under his fingers.

Every nerve in my body is on fire. Excitement rises within. I am a bottle ready to pop.

My pussy opens up wider under his ministrations.

It's like they were made for each other. His tongue. My pussy.

He sucks my clit plunging a finger into my hole at the same time. In and out, hard and soft. Maintaining the pressure as I twist and turn, my body writhing with rapture.

I almost scare myself with my loud scream of pleasure.

"My turn," he grunts.

Keeping his fingers on my clit, he stands up and plunges his cock into my clenching pussy.

I feel his body shaking as he leans over me.

I push my ass back against his dick, loving every hard stroke he's giving me.

"Baby, I can fuck you here all day."

"Do it," I dare him.

He spreads my ass cheeks and pitches deeper. I close my eyes and take it.

There's nothing better than the deep, sweet satisfaction of making my man shout my name.

His milk trickles down my leg mixing with mine. I'm a mess. And I love it.

He falls against my back, nuzzles my neck.

"Good God, woman. You're a drug."

Something inside me shifts. A heart, a womb, a space for forever. The truth hits me.

I'm going to make babies with this man. And he's here for it all.

Chapter Seventeen

Just when I think I can't take the excitement any longer, he slides wet fingers between my legs and plays with my pussy.

"What?" I cry.

"One more time," he whispers.

But it isn't just once more. By the time we're done romping

all over the deck, sexing on the chair where I straddle him, on the steps where he turns me backward and consumes me as I've never been eaten before, the sun is setting, bugs are biting, and I can barely walk.

I check my phone. "Dude, we've been going for almost five hours."

He grins. "Is that a record?"

"Are you trying to get me pregnant?"

"Duh!" he says. "Obviously."

I swat his arm. "So irresponsible."

"You said you wanted a baby. Maybe then you'll move in."

"You think?"

"I hope."

"Aren't we doing things out of order?"

"We can get married tomorrow," he says, dead serious. "But I want a big, fancy wedding. And we still have to meet your daughter, Lucy."

"Thanksgiving," I grin excitedly. "I can't believe that's happening."

"I want to meet your mom and those girlfriends of yours. And buy you a one-of-a-kind dress."

"You've got this all planned out, don't you? I'm the one who's supposed to want all the fanfare."

The truth is, I used to want all that. But I'd marry Keston on this beach without any fancy stuff.

"We're doing everything right," he says. "Besides, you're not getting pregnant yet. I know your cycle. And you're still on the pill."

"You know it all, huh?"

"When it comes to you, yes. As much as I can."

"You're weird."

"Thanks, I love you too."

Later, after we've both showered, he unpacks a whole BBQ chicken he'd brought home, which he'd almost forgotten in our quest to out-sex each other.

As we eat on the deck, fairy lights twinkling to match the starry sky, the tropical breeze lifting my hair off my shoulders, I tell him what I'm most concerned about.

"Baby, what would I do on St. Nicholas? If . . . *when* I live here?"

He wipes his fingers on a paper towel. "What do you mean? You told me your secret is to give up the lawyer life."

"That's my fantasy. I can't actually do it."

"Why not? I'll take care of you. While you figure out what you want to do, other than be my wife, have my kids, and love me forever."

I roll my eyes.

"I'll take two out of three. As long as 'love me forever' is one of them."

"Thanks. How can I say no to that?" I smile at him, licking the BBQ sauce off his fingers.

But why is life so easy for some people? They can shrug their shoulders and say, "Why not?" I'm not like that. I'm a planner.

"I've always been an independent woman. I earn my own money, be self-sufficient, and have financial security. That's hard to give up with no solid plan in mind."

"You want to make money, is that it? To buy stuff? Do stuff?" The way he says it makes me sound shallow.

Am I shallow? I suppose if you have to ask yourself that question, you probably are.

I nod miserably. "Yeah. Not that all this isn't amazing." I sweep my arm out to embrace the dark beach. "This is truly gorgeous."

"But . . . it's not enough for you to want to live here." His glum tone of voice shakes me. I'm so used to his happy-go-lucky, upbeat persona. Damn, I am a monster.

"I don't know," I whisper. "Maybe if I had something to do. Like how I helped Mrs. Harris at the museum by organizing the artifacts. Something to feel useful."

Hustling to gather my plate and napkins, he says, "Follow me."

"Where're we going?"

"First, we're washing the dishes." He tosses a cloth my way. "You can dry."

I beg him to tell me what's on his mind, but he whistles a tune and scrubs the plates clean.

"Is it a surprise?"

He ignores me. "What else do you need to live happily on St. Nicholas? Let's get it all out now. I want a happy wifey."

I swat his butt with my dish towel. "I'm not going to be the little wifey who stays at home, you know."

"A man can dream." He leans over and kisses my forehead. "Wifey. Doesn't that sound nice?"

I smirk. It does. But I'm not admitting that to him.

"Hit it," he says as he rinses salad bowls and hands them to me. "Tell me everything you need. Besides me."

I shake my head. "I love your beach house, Kes. But I'm worried it's too small for us to live in together. We'd be on top of each other all the time."

He nods, gazing at the utensils he's wiping clean.

"I'd like to contribute to our finances."

He shuts off the water. Turns to me as I dry the last fork.

"Come here."

I follow him down the tiny hall past the bedroom and bathroom to a door that looks like it's for a closet.

"What's this?"

He plucks a key from above the door frame.

"My den."

"You have a whole other room you've been keeping a secret?"

He stops turning the key and looks at me. "We could easily have more rooms. I'm working on it."

"You are?"

"What do you think I was talking to Tabitha about this morning?"

I screw up my nose. "I don't know. What?"

He was talking to Tabitha this morning!?

"She's the head of the Department of Property and Procurement. She has lots of connections with contractors all over the island."

"Oh," I say softly. "You're going to expand?"

"Yes, my dear. I can build more than tiki huts on the beach. I've already signed up for extra shifts at work to make the money to pay for it. And I am going to win that golf tournament at Christmas."

His tall body blocks the hall light. In the shadows, I feel small for not believing in him more.

"Okay," I say. "That's exciting. I want to help. Not with the golf. Financially, I mean. If I'm going to live here."

"If?" He sucks his teeth. "You're living here. And please stop saying 'finances.' No one here uses that word. Unless they work at the National Bank of St. Nicholas."

I frown. "What do you say instead?"

"We keep it simple. We say '*money*.' And for the record, I don't need your money. I will take care of you while you figure out what you want to do that makes you *happy*. Not what makes you *money*."

"You don't have to be rude about it."

He smacks my butt. Hard.

"Ouch!"

"*That* was rude. Now, move your ass."

"I swear you're gonna . . . ." I don't finish because the door swings open. Keston flicks a switch.

I can't believe my eyes.

Chapter Eighteen

The bright overhead light illuminates a room packed with boxes, crates, and old chests. Like *old*, with ornate carvings decorating the lids.

I spy what looks like a family crest, as well as plastic containers filled with old ledgers or leather-bound notebooks.

I press a hand over my heart. I hadn't expected to see much in this room. It's a shocking sight. It's more than surprising. It's like someone opened a door to a magical world.

On the far wall is a map.

"Is that St. Nicholas?" I ask.

"Yes, and surrounding islands."

I point at No Man's Land. "I can tell. This is amazing. Like walking into a time vault."

I step forward carefully so my hip doesn't bump any boxes and topple them.

"What is all of this?"

"Family stuff," he says.

"It looks like a museum. *In your house.* Does Mrs. Harris know about this?" I wag a finger at him. "She'd love to see this."

"You said you wanted something to do. And you enjoyed your work at the museum. Maybe you could . . . ."

"Yes!" I shout. I spin and throw my arms around his neck. "Yes, yes, yes!"

A smile stretches across his face. "Okay."

"Oh, my goodness. I feel like Beauty."

"Who?" He scratches his head.

"When the Beast gave her the perfect gift."

At his puzzled expression, I put my hands on my hips. "The *library?*"

No sign of understanding. I sigh.

"Never mind. This is perfect. Is it really for me? When can I start? What do you want me to do exactly?"

I'm so excited I'm rattling off questions without giving him a chance to respond.

"Who gave you all this?" I side-eye him. "How long has it been here?"

He presses both hands to either side of my face.

"Baby, it's all yours. My grandmother left it to me when she died. It's the Kips' family heritage. It's been here ever since. I don't think Mrs. Harris knows. But I thought one day I'd go through it all and give anything of historical value to the museum."

"Amazing," I say, spinning around in the small cleared-out path between the chests.

"There's more," he says slowly. He turns the large map over.

I peer closely at what appears to be a rough-cut map drawn on burlap, linen, or another cloth. Red handwriting lines the sides of it.

"Whoa!"

"Okay, don't get too excited."

"Too late," I murmur.

"This is a treasure map my father and grandfather used to search for the Kipson treasure."

"WHAT!"

"Calm down. It would be best if you didn't search for it. My father died doing just that. I wanted you to know. In case you came across anything connected to the treasure."

"Is it pirate treasure?" I feel my heart racing a million miles per hour.

He sighs. "The story passed down in my family is that many years ago, the man they called the Black Pirate King of the Caribbean was my ancestor. His name was Kipson. He lived in the late 1700s to early 1800s."

"Yes?" I modify my excitement so I can pay attention. It's not every day the man you love says, "Hey, I got a pirate treasure out there."

"Anyway," Keston says solemnly, "Kipson's son grew up on the pirate boat with his father. As an adult, he came to St. Nicholas and bought land. A lot of it." Keston indicates outside to the beach and forest.

"But because he was . . . a pirate's son, or because he was of a mixed race, he wasn't allowed a deed for the land. But . . ."

I suck my teeth.

"He got a woman high up in the island government to purchase it for him, and she then granted him the deeds for all of this."

"High up?"

"She was married to the Governor."

"Why would she do that for him?"

Keston shrugs. "I don't know if it's true. The story is that he was her son."

I plop down on the dusty floor. "You have got to be kidding me. Do you mean Alex's story is true? It's not a myth. The Scottish princess loved the Black Pirate of the Caribbean?"

"I think she was just a noblewoman. The story grew and turned her into a princess. You know how rumors escalate."

"What does all that have to do with a pirate treasure?"

He leans against the door and crosses his arms. "In one of the journals," he indicates the boxes and chests, "there is mention of two treasures. One is hidden in plain sight 'with all the beauty man could want.'" He looks shy. "I'm quoting it."

"Go on."

"I think that treasure is this land. This property goes on farther than you can see. Down the beach with fruit trees, a river, and a waterfall."

I blink. *And he doesn't have a clothes dryer?*

A long silence passes. Keston's eyes grow shiny.

"You don't have to tell me." I stand up and hug him. "It's okay."

My inner voice is howling, "What the fuck! We want to know!"

He wipes a corner of his eye. I lay my head on his chest.

His large hand strokes my hair. "The other treasure is still out there. It's hidden 'where joy and sorrow lie side by side.'"

"Are you quoting again?"

"Yes. My father was obsessed with finding it. We're land rich but poor in terms of . . . *money*. He wanted to fix that."

"Why not sell your land or some of it?" I ask the obvious question.

He leans back and scowls. "No. My ancestors bought this with their blood, sweat, and tears. Kipson had to escape slavery, become a pirate king, and do God knows what else. And who knows what his son endured. Our family will never sell it. To have a developer build condos or a hotel? No thanks."

"Got it." I've never heard Keston speak so passionately about anything other than me.

"You never have to sell your land," I promise him. I swear an oath to myself that I will uphold that vow.

"So, what now? I'm happy to organize it. Inventory the books and artifacts."

He straightens up. "Thank you."

"Nice. So, can I at least *think* about the hidden treasure? Imagine what fresh eyes might do with old clues."

"Oh no," he smack his forehead. "Not you, too. Treasure hunting is addictive. I should know."

I kiss his lips. "You are my treasure," I whisper.

"That's better."

"But imagine if . . ."

I'm already imagining all the stuff we could do. Expand the house. Buy an SUV to traverse the rough roads. Travel to New York to see my daughter a lot. Open Keston's dream bar.

"You're already spending that pirate treasure in your head, aren't you?" he teases.

I gulp. "Maybe."

He pulls me close to his chest. Wraps both of his muscled

arms around me and looks into my eyes. "Do you think this will give you something to do? For a while? So you won't leave me?"

I nod vigorously. "Oh, definitely. Especially if I find more clues to the hidden treasure."

He groans, "Don't start."

Chapter Nineteen

I toss and turn all night.

You'd think with all the sweet lovemaking I'm stocking up on, I'd fall asleep the moment my head hit the pillow.

No luck.

My dream self is trapped in a room of boxes that creak open

and shut. The boxes morph into dark, rounded caves that appear and disappear.

The caves are in the sea. Waves smack against pointy rocks at the caves' openings. I follow a shadowy form resembling Captain Jack Sparrow with wavy hair and a silver sword.

When he turns around, it's Keston, but even more handsome (if possible), with a feverish gleam in his eyes. One green, one grey. He grips a handful of gold coins. I can barely hear his whispers, "There's more where this came from. Follow me."

As I start following him again, he stops and turns around. "Do you know where we're going?"

I shake my head.

He grips my shoulder. "It's a secret. Tell no one."

His face is gone. It's a smooth, blank nothing. I scream.

I pop up into a sitting position. The real-life Keston pulls me back down and cradles me against his chest. I poke him to make sure he's not part of my dream.

"Ouch, woman."

Okay, he's real.

I close my eyes and try to sleep.

By morning, I'm exhausted from my dreams.

"What was wrong last night, baby?" Keston asks as he pulls down his Cocoa Reef Resort polo shirt over his washboard abs.

"I was having the same dream. Over and over. You were in it. But it wasn't you." I don't want to tell him it was him, but as a cuter swashbuckling pirate.

How old am I again?

I pull on one of his t-shirts and follow him out to the sun-drenched porch. Mist rises off the dewy grass in the distance.

You know who is munching on the grass.

"She's back." I point at the grey and white donkey.

"I think she has a thing for you." Keston smothers a laugh. "She didn't start showing up every day until you arrived."

"Hmm," I grunt. "Why does she steal my clothes and not yours?"

"Yours are nicer."

I scrub sleep from my eyes and kiss him goodbye.

"Be safe," I say as he cranks up his rusty motorcycle.

"Be fierce," he shouts over the noise.

"Fierce?"

"That's what you were mumbling in your sleep. "Be fierce.""

"Really? I don't remember that. Did I say anything else?"

He plunks down his helmet. "No. Wait. You were mumbling, 'Where is it?' over and over."

"Where is what?"

He snorts. "That's what I wondered. Good thing you didn't say, 'Where is he?' I'd have woken you right up. Find out who '*he*' is."

I roll my eyes. "Jealous of my dream man?"

"If it walks like a duck and talks like a duck . . . ."

"It's a *dream* duck!" I shout.

He revs the engine. "That's how they start. The sneaky bastards."

He grins and throws me a kiss. "Call me if you want to head out."

"Why?"

"I'll send a car to pick you up."

"Maybe I'll ride your bike." I point to the rusted bicycle with wide tires and a black wire basket on the front. Like the motorcycle, the bike's seen better days.

"Ha! You're better off riding the donkey through the trails than that thing."

I roll my eyes. I can't with this man and his cheerfulness so early in the morning.

The donkey brays loudly, agreeing it's better than an old bicycle.

"Fine. I'll keep that in mind."

An hour later, it's barely eight-thirty, and I'm sheltering under the broad porch umbrella, washed, dressed, and sipping lemongrass iced tea made with freshly squeezed limes from Keston's trees. The lime gives the tea a boost of Vitamin C and a kick of acid.

The sun is doing its tropical dance across the morning sky, brightening the day like a kid with a popsicle. I don't think I will ever get used to how fast night and day arrive here.

One minute, the sun is setting in a glory of orangey colors; the next minute, it has bailed, and the entire sky is in total darkness.

Caribbean daybreak is the same. It behaves like your one friend who doesn't have any chill. "Wake up already, I'm fucking HERE!"

But this sunshine and limey iced tea provide the energy I need to begin my attack on the boxes.

It's not as if I have a job.

Not worrying about money or where it'll come from may work for Keston. He's following his passion for being a mixologist, creating new drink recipes, and bringing joy to stressed-out vacationers.

But not everyone is born knowing what their passion is.
Like me.

I don't have any natural talents. For forty years, I've gone to school and followed the professional path my mother encouraged: doctor, lawyer, or engineer. I chose a lawyer.

With a father who is a painter and a mom who is an English

professor, we never had much money growing up. "Finances," or lack of them, drove a wedge between my parents.

So, although Keston urges me not to worry about making money, it's hard to ignore. Mom insisted I choose a profession that paid well so I would not have to struggle in life. Now, Keston is asking me to undo a lifetime of beliefs.

My most profound belief is that if I don't hustle, I'll die.

But, *would* I die?

Not according to Keston who says he will take care of me.

A loud braying interrupts my thoughts.

"I didn't ask you," I holler in the direction of the donkey. "And leave my clothes alone."

Silence.

"*Please.*"

I tidy the kitchen, check emails, and heart my girlfriends' latest Insta posts. Then, I meander down the hallway toward the den.

I never asked myself what I wanted to do. Is it too late for that?

Maybe when you reach forty, you're supposed to stick with what you've invested all your time and education into, making the best of the life you created.

"*Hee-haw.*"

Or not!

A racket outside diverts my attention from the philosophical question of what to do with my short, precious life on earth.

"What is it?" I sigh, heading out the front door into the scorching sunshine.

The annoying donkey trots across the dirt road straight toward Keston's porch.

"Shoo!" I yell, waving my hands about like I'm a human scarecrow.

If I were in my office in midtown Manhattan, I would not be yelling at any donkeys right now—something to consider.

The donkey stares at me with its big, slanted eyes. I must admit it's cute. A hint of mischief shines through its tilted eyelashes like it's daring me to do something.

I shake my phone at her.

It shakes its head back, sending a ripple through the black mohawk growing between its ears.

I hate to call Keston at work. I need to handle this situation.

Hmmmm. Where does this animal live anyway? Is it unhoused? Should I put up flyers to locate its owners? And if it has owners, why haven't they built a fence to keep it in?

"Where's your mommy and daddy?" I ask it.

The donkey stares me down like we're playing poker, trying to guess my next move.

"It's no secret," I assure the donkey from the porch, keeping a safe distance from its front and back hooves. "I want to get you to the right person. So, you'll be happy, and I'll be . . . *happier* you're not eating my clothing."

I get nothing back. Just a long, soulful gaze taking me in.

"Why are you watching me like that? What do you think this would be like? You and me cuddling up and watching Netflix together?"

The donkey kicks its heels, spins, and heads toward the clothesline.

"Don't you dare!" I raise a fist.

My threat is as meaningless as the donkey's remorse.

In seconds, it clamps ginormous teeth around the hem of my jeans, dragging it from the line.

Oh, hell no.

I grab the first thing my hand finds—Keston's t-shirt, which has been left here since yesterday's lovemaking.

"Shoo! Go away!"

I run down the steps but stop at the edge of the yard.

We have a standoff.

The donkey hee-haws at me. I wave the t-shirt like a matador with a raging bull.

The donkey grins maniacally, its teeth lined up like a white picket fence.

It seems to say, "I was here before you, missy."

"Go! Get!" I shake the T-shirt in front of its face.

The donkey drops my jeans, and I grab them off the sand.

"Go home," I shout hopefully at the grey and white animal. It trots down the dirt road, its backside swaying, its white-tipped tail flicking the air, like it's saying, "Get a life, woman."

"You and me both," I mutter.

I hurry into the house, clutching my jeans to my chest. I'm sure I feel donkey saliva on my denim.

Ewww!

If nothing else, that face-off has my blood pumping. To say I'm scared to get bitten by the donkey is an understatement.

Although Keston promised it wouldn't hurt me. His exact words were, "Jesus rode a wild donkey into Jerusalem in the New Testament. I think this one is fine."

"Have you seen those teeth?" I'd countered.

Chapter Twenty

Igather up cleaning supplies and several large trash bags.

The door to the den creaks open, reminding me of my dream. I hold my breath, expecting a real skeleton to appear.

Last night with Keston by my side, it didn't look creepy. Now, with the blackout curtains blocking the sunshine, shadowy shapes lurking in the corners, and a ticking noise resounding somewhere in the house, I'm reconsidering my plans to dive in.

This looks like a Stephen King story about to be told. With me as the naïve main character.

I step gingerly along the narrow path between the piled-high boxes made by Keston last night.

Unfortunately, pulling open the curtains is a no-no. Dust sits like a second skin on what I thought was brown fabric. Who knows what color they are underneath the grime?

I have a new plan. I'll take one box at a time out to the porch and open it there, where it's bright and cheery and dust-free.

And hopefully donkey-free too.

The only problem is that the chests with the carved lids that look the most promising are way too heavy for me to carry or even drag to the porch.

Something tells me I need to start with them to unearth the most promising ancestral goodies—clues to the hidden treasure.

I cross my arms and tap my foot. Time for Plan B.

A loud braying noise catapults me almost out of my sandals.

I smack a hand on my forehead. "Not again!"

"Hee-haw!"

I march to the front door ready to do battle.

One turn of the knob and I'm staring into the donkey's face.

"*Arrrrh!*" I scream scudding backwards. "What are you doing in the house?" Technically, it's the porch, but close enough.

The donkey bares its teeth in a smile. I must be in shock because I notice specks of blue on its coat and a faint stripe running down its back. It smells of fresh grass and sunshine. With a slight musky undertone.

"What in God's name are you wearing on your head? Is that my . . . *hat*?"

My beautiful hat, which Keston bought for me the first day we went to town, is perched between the donkey's pointy ears. Silky ribbons trail to the ground, as if waiting to be tied under its chin.

"You've got to be kidding me."

I grab my phone out of my back pocket as I step back into the hall.

"He'll never believe me. Don't move." I glare at the donkey.

I quickly snap a couple of shots to send to Keston while keeping one eye on the animal still standing on the porch like a visitor waiting to be invited in.

The donkey gives me its left profile and preens, buck teeth bared wide.

"What should I do?" I text to Keston.

Maybe now he'll finally realize the problem and do something.

My phone pings. Keston's response is three laughing-on-the-floor emojis.

I stare at them aghast. Does he not understand the severity of this situation? Am I overreacting? I don't think so. I doubt anyone in St. Nicholas has a donkey hanging out on their front porch.

"She looks cute in your hat," he texts back.

"We need to contain her somehow. She's wearing my hat and looking at me."

"What do you have in mind?"

I think for a moment. "Can we call animal control?"

A rolling eye emoji. "The entire island will laugh at us."

"Hee-haw," the donkey brays at me. Like it's saying, "They'd laugh at *you*."

The hat tilts precariously, ready to slide off the black mohawk hair.

"Kes, how do I get her off the porch at least?"

"I'll come home soon. Can you close the door and ignore her for now?"

"I'll try." But I feel bad he's coming home just for this. My fingers ache typing out the next words. "I'll handle it. You don't worry about me."

Meanwhile, *I'm* worried about me.

"You sure? I don't mind. I can pop over there in no time."

I shake my head as I type out, "No, I'll be okay." I hope I sound convincing. Optimism is not my forte.

"Call me if you need me, babe. I'm not far away. Or I can have Dex shoot over there."

Oh, my goodness. I'd look like a diva. Making a big commotion over nothing. I assure him I'll be fine.

I slide the phone into my pocket. Bite my bottom lip with determination.

"It's you or me," I address the donkey, whose ears perk up even taller than usual. "One of us must go. And it won't be me."

She gives a mournful bray.

"I'm not falling for it," I say sternly.

Another long crying noise escapes its mouth. She looks pitifully at me. Her white-tipped tail swishes then hangs limply.

"I'm sorry. But you're a nuisance. And I want my hat."

Before the donkey can defend itself, my phone pings again.

Keston has sent a cute donkey emoji and a heart with a text message.

"I'm sorry you're dealing with this situation on your own, babe. Try to ignore her. Or better yet, embrace her. What we push away the hardest is what we attract the most."

What the hell does that mean?

I text back, "You want me to embrace it? Are you mad?"

"It's a donkey, not a weapon of mass destruction."

"Sometimes I really don't like you.'

"That's okay, I always love you."

I send a rolling eyes emoji and drop my phone on the window ledge.

Okay, CJ, you're on your own. With fingers pressed to the sides of my face, I take deep breaths.

"Yo," I say as fearlessly as possible.

The donkey blinks.

It has a stubbornness I admire.

"How are you with hauling boxes to the porch?"

Chapter Twenty-One

It takes a bit of maneuvering, but I manage to get the animal inside the house. I hold out a carrot stick. I assume donkeys are like horses and will eat carrots.

I approach her with caution.

She backs away.

I step forward.

She backs up further. My hat teeters on her head, ready to hit the floor.

I reach for it. The donkey brays loudly, and I jump.

But then, it bows and tilts its head to the side, toppling the hat from between its pointy ears into my open hands.

"Wow! That was brilliant," I praise her.

She grins a large white donkey smile that would put one of Denzel Washington's smiles to shame.

"We have a lot in common," I tell her. "I don't know anyone else here. We can be friends. I hope you like the name 'Trixie.' I will call you that because you tricked me into liking you."

"Hee-haw." She seems to agree.

Keston wants me to embrace the donkey. Well, that's what I'm doing. Emotionally.

I hope he didn't mean *physically*.

I gaze at the donkey doing a sideways trot down the hall as I lead with the carrot. "You look like you just left a bar. You've got that shuffle thing going on."

She flicks her ears at me. Flashes a big smile. I make a note to Google how intelligent donkeys are. I swear Trixie understands what I'm saying.

"By the way, I'm Carmela Jones. But I go by CJ to my friends."

Trixie brays.

"Cool."

She shakes her rump. Followed by batting her long dark eyelashes.

"I get it. You want attention. Okay, may I say what a pretty donkey you are?"

The animal stares quietly waiting for me to say more.

"Trixie, enough with the compliments. I need help moving

heavy boxes from inside this room to the front porch. Are you up for that?"

Her loud bray tells me she is.

I think.

Using common sense that I didn't know I had and my newfound ability to talk to animals, well, to this particular donkey, I managed to haul two of the largest chests to the porch with just a few scratches to Keston's walls.

The entire enterprise involved a rope I found in his kitchen cupboard that I tied around one chest at a time. The other end was tied around a makeshift saddle and harness I made for Trixie out of a blanket and belts. I dangled carrots to motivate Trixie to keep pulling.

Sweat ran down my face as if I was the one doing the pulling instead of the dangling. But alas, I was set up outside where I felt brave enough to tackle the contents of the old chests. Come what may.

Trixie lay on the grass right next to the porch, keeping me company like an oversized lumpy grey dog. Occasionally, I'd throw her another carrot to keep her happy after all of her hard work.

I open my laptop, create a spreadsheet, and begin inventorying the first chest. Like all new relationships, the honeymoon period of excitement and newness quickly wore off.

Three hours later, I'm sweating, my back aches, and my fingers are numb from thumbing through endless papers.

The first chest is about four feet deep. I reach the bottom at last and sigh.

Be careful what you wish for. I could be in a hammock reading a book instead of being "useful!"

It's not until I'm halfway through the second chest with the family crest on its lid that I find something of interest.

"Whoa, Trix, I think we found something important."

Gentle snores and not-so-gentle farts emanate from Trixie, who is lying on the grass.

I turn my attention back to what is in my hands—a soft, buttery, old leather diary. It appears to be older than anything I've come across so far.

I pull on gloves I found in Keston's kitchen. To protect it from oil on my fingers, as Mrs. Harris taught me.

I forget my aches and pains. The leather is dark brown with an intricate embossed pattern showing scuff marks and deep creases.

I open the journal carefully. The pages inside are unevenly cut with a ragged textured edge as if they were made by hand.

Some of the pages retain their original cream color, but most of the pages are yellowed and some have brown age spots. The binding is sewn with thick thread.

"Oh my," I breathe when I see the first page and the date.

"Diary of Ms. Charlotte Campbell, twenty years old."

Below that is written "1803."

It's a diary! More than *two hundred years old.*

The name rings a bell. Is "Campbell" a name Keston mentioned?

Then it hits me. At the museum. A plantation log by a Scottish person whose last name was Campbell was on display.

But who is this, Charlotte Campbell? Was she a family member of the plantation owner?

Chapter Twenty-Two

The handwriting inside the journal is an elegant, flowing script. Pressed on the inside of the journal is an old flower. It slides out on a swatch of tartan, giving me *Braveheart* vibes.

Wow! Charlotte Campbell from Scotland lived on St. Nicholas Island in 1803.

I turn the pages slowly, my fingers encased in the plastic gloves. My heart thumps in my chest loudly in anticipation of what I'll find here.

Dark blots and smudges fill the first few pages as if the writer is getting used to her ink pen and new book.

My eyes travel down the long lines of flowery script. Ms. Charlotte had plenty to say. At least to her diary. I try reading a few pages. It's tedious. The words may be English but in an archaic style that is not easy to translate. Kind of like Shakespeare.

Trying to decipher it will take a long time at least for me.

I turn the pages one by one, skimming the text for any other names or dates, to determine who Ms. Charlotte Campbell was and how she fit into St. Nicholas's life.

The diary details her walks in the garden, observations of birds on the trees, and tiny drawings of a coconut tree leaning over the sea. Then, as I flip the pages, a name catches my eye— more than catches my eye; it rips the air right out of my lungs.

I place a hand on my chest to calm myself down. I forget the sun in the sky. The waves crashing on the shore, the parrots screeching, and the donkey snoring. I almost forget myself.

I'm transported to 1803.

I'm sitting on a porch, on an island in the Caribbean, but hundreds of years ago. I feel the same balmy air Charlotte Campbell wrote about. I hear the same birds. I taste the same tangy salt in the air.

I *am* Charlotte Campbell.

The hairs on my arms stand up. A tingle zings up my spine. My poor throat croaks with dryness.

Across the page, written in clear, precise handwriting, different than the flowery script from earlier, are the words,

"*My Kipson.*" Written three times.

I can barely stop my hands from shaking as I read aloud:

Upon this day, it is my expectation that my Kipson shall make his arrival. In anticipation, I shall patiently abide at that precise confluence where the river doth embrace the vast sea. It is there, where the trio of stones are so meticulously arranged as to resemble the gaping maw of a fearsome dragon, and the copse of trees beyond stand as the very likeness of its coiled tail, that I shall eagerly await his presence.

My eyes race ahead, past how she plans to traverse the rutted roads, which gown she will don, how she will arrange her hair.

God, she's worse than me. My breath catches at the next sentence:

His bounty, secure in its repose, remains steadfastly where he, with great secrecy, hath consigned it. There, amidst the whispers of the untamed wilderness, it shall reside in perpetuity, undisturbed and enduring as the very sands of time.

My eyes bulge. What bounty? A secret consignment? In the wild?

I scan the pages quickly as my heart gallops along. Could this be a hoax? Then, my eyes alight on prized words.

"Prized?" Ha! I sound like Charlotte in my head. Or whoever this 19th-century woman was that wrote about Mr. Kipson.

I read her words as if I were a woman from that time.

I would sooner embrace the cold kiss of death itself than betray the sanctity of that most clandestine spot, the resting place of a pirate's treasure of old.

I place the old journal carefully on the table and scream into my hands. *"Ahhhhh!"*

Trixie leaps up with a, "What!" expression in her dark, expressive eyes.

I leap into the air, hopping on one foot and then the other. I spin, I do a crazy dance. I cover my mouth with both hands again and scream to the parrots flying above.

"We're going to find pirate treasure. We're going to be rich. I can quit my job. I can move here. I can . . . ."

I look at Trixie who is staring intently at my mad antics.

"Marry Keston and have a family," I end with a whisper because that is my dream. Even if I don't give voice to it often.

I've had a career as a lawyer. I've just found my daughter given up for adoption at birth, or she found me, and we're going to be reunited.

All I want now is my own little family. And to know my birth child. Is that too much to ask?

I eye the Universe and cringe. "Maybe also a truck with big tires to drive down the dirt roads?"

Trixie hee-haws and wanders off. Which is a sign for me to calm down.

The beach in front of me looks like an untamed wilderness today. Imagine it in the 1800s. It must have been a wild, wild West, with missionaries, pirates, and colonizers fighting over land and people, their gold and souls—not necessarily in that order.

I drum my pen against the paper and tap my foot to the same rhythm.

Scattered clouds float against a cobalt blue sky. A shower of purple bougainvillea intertwines with sun-yellow daffodils, creating their own natural bouquet on the bushes bordering the porch.

I shake my head in wonder. Paradise can be beautiful *and* scary.

Like this mystery. It's vast and intense, I feel unequal to the task. I don't know how Charlotte kept the secret of the island's bounty a secret. Or did she?

I can't wait to tell Kesotn.

Based on how he reacted last night, it's not going to be the best news! He's already lost his father somehow. I can't blame Keston for wanting to dodge another potential treasure-hunting bullet.

Trixie and I will have to break it to him gently.

Because I have a gut feeling that the treasure is still out there.

Everybody wants the good. Not the bad or the ugly.

Although all three are usually wrapped up together. Finding the treasure would be amazing. How we get to it, not so much.

"Trixie, dear, I thought *you* were the bad and the ugly. But guess what? You're the good."

"Hee-haw," my new donkey friend brays loudly. I laugh at her. Tangles of fuchsia bougainvillea wrap around her ears and trail down to her chin.

"How'd you do that?" I ask admiringly. "I can barely keep one hibiscus flower tucked behind my ear."

Trixie lets out an ungodly fart.

Damn, girl.

That's life for you. Just when you think you've got it figured out, it shows up in a different way.

Chapter Twenty-Three

I'm not ready to climb on Trixie's back and test the homemade saddle and reins.

I pat her shoulder. "Maybe one day, I'll ride you around. But, I need more time, you understand?

She brays at me.

I don't think all the time in the world will get me up on a donkey's back.

"You never know," I assure my new friend.

I pedal furiously down the dirt road and then across the short track toward the Cocoa Reef Resort. Keston is on his second shift, so he'll still be there.

I can take a shower at the villa, then hang out at the bar with him. What I really want to do is curl up with the diary, deciphering old English and looking for clues to the pirate treasure.

I breathe a sigh of relief upon entering the luxurious villa. I also feel guilty. I'm way too excited to be in this marble palace with gilt-edged faucets, thick, creamy rugs, and a bed as large as Keston's entire home.

I spin around like Cinderella entering the castle. I have a golf cart to drive around instead of a donkey. I have room service and a pool. I have housekeeping if I want it and laundry service.

Thank goodness. Okay, maybe I'm a bit shallow because I prefer the villa to roughing it daily.

Can't I have both? Luxury and simplicity. Some days, it's great to be pampered. Other days . . . okay, I *always* want to be pampered. But I'm willing to compromise between super pampered and regular pampered.

After a long hot shower under the rain shower head built for two, I wrap up in a thick towel and make a cup of tea from the sideboard filled with goodies.

My backpack sits on the edge of the bed waiting to be unpacked. The diary is safely tucked away inside, in several layers of plastic cling wrap. My plan had been to copy it at the front desk so I could put the original back in the chest.

But the front desk doesn't have a copier that would work for something like this. Plus, I'd have to give the book to the receptionist to do it, and I'm not parting with Charlotte Campbell's diary.

I unwrap the diary and open it up on the white duvet. Using my iPhone's camera, I begin snapping photos of the pages. It takes a long time to turn each one carefully then center it and snap a good photo.

By the time I'm done, it's after eight. My stomach growls like a demon. I've ignored several text messages from Keston. It's time to go find him and explain.

When I zoom up to the beach bar in the golf cart, Bob Marley's song, *Jammin'*, is playing over invisible speakers tucked into the surrounding trees and bushes. Guests swarm the bar like it's happy hour at spring break.

"What's going on?" I ask Dex, Keston's assistant, as he hurries by with a tray of drinks for a table in a private gazebo.

He grins at me. "Keston is a genius. He's making brand-new cocktails. And getting people to vote on them. Grab your card." Dex points to a table where a woman is handing out clipboards and pens.

"Oh." I tiptoe to peek over the shoulders and heads blocking the bar. "Cool."

It feels weird to be so close to Keston and not hug or kiss him after being apart all day. But he's surrounded by fifty people all shouting his name and raising glasses and singing his praises. No way he'll see me in the back of the crowd.

But then the crowd parted. I had a direct line of sight to the wooden tiki bar, with fresh limes in the hanging baskets.

Keston's handsome face appears between the opening in the crowd. He's tall enough to tower over most of the people there. His curls are sticking up, a bandana tied around them making him look like a pirate, or maybe I just have pirates on the brain.

"He's so good at what he does," a woman near me sighs.

"And so gorgeous. I could eat him for breakfast," another woman laughs.

Whoa!

"If looks could kill I'd skewer his hot girlfriend right now," a third woman in the crew remarks. All three stare longingly in Keston's direction.

What the fuck? I'm his girlfriend. Me!

But no one is looking at me. They're all staring at a bar stool, where lo and behold, sits a woman whose bare back I do not recognize.

Well, I recognize it isn't *mine*!

And what is my so-called boyfriend doing?

My Keston is leaning across the bar, talking to the sexy usurper of boyfriends. His white-toothed smile gleams like a crescent moon, the same way he smiles at me.

A knife twists inside my gut. Is this what happens when I'm not around?

Of course, dummy. He's a hot bartender . . . I mean, a *mixologist* at a resort. His job is literally to entertain and make people happy. He told me once he had a "bartender" spiel.

It sure is working. Ms. Sexy Back is ready to fall in his lap. Her body language is obvious.

Watching how easy it is for Keston to flirt with another woman makes the smug super confidence I've been feeling about us vanish like a genie into thin air.

All this time, I've been weighing whether I should stay in St. Nicholas and build a life with Keston, and he's been lining up options.

I can feel my imagination running way off course, but I can't wield it back in.

Not with the image of gorgeous women swooning over him right in front of my face.

Any insecurities I have are gathered together doing the *Electric Slide* in the rational part of my brain.

But can I blame him? When he asks me to move in, I balk. When he tries to make plans, I hesitate.

All to give myself space. Because the decision to move to an island with a different culture, history, and lifestyle is scary.

I feel like such a fool. Telling myself I need more space in his house. I can't live without a washer/dryer. I'd like a cappuccino machine and a SUV.

When the only thing I really want and need is him, now it may be too late.

Chapter Twenty-Four

"Get a grip," I yell at my subconscious trying to derail me.

That woman is probably some beautiful guest who is leaving tomorrow. You're here for three more weeks. *At least.*

Three weeks in which to find that pirate treasure. To present Keston with his family legacy.

We can still have it all. Money plus love. Okay, not in *that* order, right, CJ?

"Right!"

I gaze into the tall cocktail glass Dex has placed in my hand. He said something about it being number seven on the list.

"This better be good," I mutter to no one. "After the day I've had . . . am still having . . . I need the best damn rum drink."

"Oh, it's good," a deep voice whispers in my ear.

I shriek. Almost drop the drink.

"What?" I spin around to see Keston. Legs wide, arms crossed, looking like he stepped out of Wakanda.

I want to toss the drink and throw my arms around his neck. But I can't start behaving weird and . . . *jealous.*

Let's call it what it is. My heart is spinning in my chest cavity trying to find a safe place to land.

"Well?" he smirks. "Is it the best damn rum drink?"

I stir the liquid with the cute umbrella and cherry perched at the side. I lock eyes with him under my lashes as I slowly sip the turquoise concoction. My eyes open wide.

"This is incredible."

He grins. "Thanks."

"No, really Keston. This is your best yet." I mean it. I suck down the rest of the cocktail forgetting it's loaded with rum.

"What's in it?"

"I could tell you . . . but then."

"*Whatever.*" I roll my eyes. "I'll bear the consequences."

"You'd have to marry me."

I press a hand against my chest. Is he serious?

Then I see all eyes on us. "Oh, is this part of your bartender spiel? It's a joke?"

He laughs and pulls me toward him. He removes the glass from my hands and places it on a table.

"Woman, I missed you." He kisses the top of my head while people stare with their tongues hanging out.

"Is he like . . . *available*?" asks the woman who said she'd eat him for breakfast.

He says clearly, "Not anymore."

I wrap my arms around his waist. "That's right. Not anymore."

I bury my head against his warm chest. Inhale his outdoorsy scent of coconut, rum, and lime.

"Baby," he says, leaning back. "I could hold you all night, but I've got to get back to the bar."

"Oh," I step backward. "Sorry. I have to tell you something important."

"What is it?"

I fast whisper behind my hand. "I found a diary in a chest. It mentions the pirate treasure."

I'm trying to be nonchalant and keep the excitement out of my voice, but my jumping up and down may give me away.

He stops walking and turns troubled eyes on me.

Then he sighs. "Okay. You have my support. But seriously, *clues*?"

I nod. "Yes! The treasure definitely exists. According to Charlotte Campbell."

He freezes. "I know her."

"You do?"

He nods. "She was the woman allegedly involved with the deeds to the Kipson land."

I blink. Loud voices clamor for more drinks. I ignore them and focus on Keston.

"I know you have to go back to the bar. But I think she was in love with Kipson."

He nods. "I've heard some of this before." He kisses my hand. "Come with me," he says, walking toward the bar.

I follow him quietly. Meanwhile, I'm shouting inside, "Yipee. I'm going to find a pirate treasure."

"Calm down, CJ," my voice of reason shows up like a hose at a fire. "This isn't *Outer Banks*."

Chapter Twenty-Five

The rest of the night passes by in a blur. Keston has a tablet open on the counter.

He's designing cocktails, recording the ingredients, and taking photos of his masterpieces.

Meanwhile, I help by keeping track of the scores. Opening a

Google spreadsheet on my phone, I type fast as people drink and rate the cocktails.

It's easy. Almost every cocktail is a 5, the best.

One very tipsy man shouts, "They're all a ten!"

I would agree, except I've decided to stick to only one drink.

"What's this all for?" I ask when Keston takes a short breather to restock the different rums.

So far, I've noted coconut rum, spiced rum, aged rum, and, of course, the best, *St. Nicholas Pirate Rum.*

I swear everyone on St. Nicholas is invested in the island's pirate history. From their regattas to the names of their beaches and coves to their alcohol.

Which gives me an idea. If Keston doesn't want to search for the pirate treasure for himself, we could look for it to give to the island.

It would help with road repairs and school facilities. Imagine how many people would come to the museum to learn about the island's history and see the actual treasure.

It would put this tiny spot in the Caribbean Sea on the map for good.

The night air grows more flower-infused as the hubbub of voices intensifies. Islanders arrive and mingle with the resort guests, forgetting they must work tomorrow.

"Someone passed the word around, Kes," Dex says, returning for more cocktails. "They're calling tonight Keston's Kreations with two Ks."

Keston beams. "Are they now?"

The fishermen are leaning on the counter and waving at me, all cleaned and dressed, hair combed, and shirt collars pressed.

"Hi, Captain Shaq," I call out.

"Is that you Starr?"

My mouth drops open at how clean-cut they look. Not a netted shirt or rough beard in sight.

Keston's hands are flying. His phone slips and falls as he tries to take a photo of a lineup of rum cocktails.

I grab his phone off the floor. It's in a protective waterproof case, so it's fine. "You make the drinks. I'll take the photos."

"Get great pictures. I need them for something."

"For what?" I ask again. "What is this all for?"

He doesn't answer; he gives me a shy smile. "You'll see."

I watch, fascinated, as he bobs from one end of the bar to another, examining bottles, choosing the perfect ingredient, and measuring the right amount of it.

It's like watching a master chef. Or an artist choosing the right paint from his color palette.

"I never realized how complicated being a mixologist can be."

He whips around, "It's fun. Not complicated."

A slew of visitors rotating in and out of the bar, clutching his beautiful drinks and smiling broadly, offer their opinions on the combinations.

"It's life-changing. Just not in the way you'd expect," a guest shouts.

"I agree," I tell Keston. "Look how you've brought all these different people together in a bonding experience."

"Keston's rum drinks for life," someone shouts as if agreeing with me.

"Oh my." I burst out laughing. "Sounds like we should make shirts with that logo."

I barely have time to sneak in a couple of photos of the red swirly drink with the orange slices looking like hot sunsets before Dex grabs them to distribute to customers.

Apparently, there's an all-you-can-drink charge paid upfront. And everyone is getting their money's worth.

"Dude, you're moving too fast," I grumble at Keston.

He kisses my nose just before he slides to the other end of

the bar as if there's a piano on the floor, and he's playing all the keys.

"Keep up, CJ. We're on a mission."

"Who lit a fire in your pants?" I ask.

"You," he smirks. "Always."

Dex returns with empty glasses and drops them in a sink of bubbly water at the back of the bar. "Next time we're having one of your all-you-can-drink nights, please ask them to hire more staff."

Keston puts his hands together and does a Namaste bow at Dex. "Sorry. I didn't think it would be so popular."

He turns to whip up something blue-green and frosty-looking, adding bitters and a secret ingredient. It's secret because the bottle has no label.

"What's this called?" I ask as he hands me a glass of the frosty blue drink.

"Don't you remember this, sweetie? I created it just for you."

I shake my head.

He stops in his tracks and crosses his arms. Biceps, triceps, and all the other *ceps* pop out.

"The day after you arrived at Cocoa Reef Resort, you were mad at me. I walked down the beach to give this to you, and you thought I was trying to poison you."

The memory of his hot body striding across the sand, calf muscles rippling, drink in hand, flashes through my head. "Your apology drink? Yes, I recall."

"You never forgave me." He turns around to make more frosty blue drinks.

I don't answer because I'm too busy siping the delicious, cool, tropical gem.

"Well, what's the name of my apology drink?"

I scribble a ten and make a smiley face with the zero in my ten.

"It's one to five, babe." Keston peeps over my shoulder. "But I'll take it, thank you. And it's called . . . ." He puts a hand to his chin. "Frosty Mermaid. Just like my baby."

"*Frosty Mermaid*?" I scowl. "Since when am I . . . ."

"Cold?" he asks, both eyebrows rising to his bandana. "Icy? Chilly?"

"Yeah, whatever. Just make more, please."

"Exactly."

"Good thing I love you," I mutter under my breath.

He slides past me with two more drinks for Dex. "Good thing I love you too."

I sip my next Frosty Mermaid as if I am a scientist taste-testing a food sample. I want to help Keston perfect his creations even if he won't tell me why he's making them.

My little frosty heart does cartwheels of happiness.

It's amazing how this man has me giddy with love. I could float right off his stool.

Or does he have me drunk with love, as Beyoncé sings?

Either way, I join the crowd singing along to Bob Marley. Because the best way to enjoy rum is with a little bit (or a lot) of reggae.

<h1 style="text-align:center">Chapter Twenty-Six</h1>

J ust as Keston and I are sailing along full of love and good vibes, along comes a gale force wind, in the form of a tall, golden-brown goddess, to rock the boat.

"Darling," gushes Tabitha St. Clair, lounging her body against the bar, one hip sticking out with a slim hand resting on it. Golden bangles jingle and chime whenever she flings her hand about, which is like every second.

"What a fabulous event. I told you it would be a success. And it is."

When did she tell him that? How come I didn't know about it? I stick the straw back in my mouth and suck on it for dear life so I don't say anything I'll regret.

"Thanks, Tabby." Keston slides a Frosty Mermaid her way and she eyes it like it's a keg of dynamite.

"*Tabby? Errrg.*"

"Darling, you know I don't do *sugarrrrr*." She rolls the "r" out so her mouth is all pouty and cute. Like the rest of her in a stunning iridescent mini dress.

I try my best not to roll my eyes.

When Keston slides down to the other end of the bar, Tabitha tilts her head and says, "You always look ready to rumble. Is that a New York thing?"

"Mmm, sure." I don't usually get intimidated easily, but this woman is Keston's friend. Who helped him through his ordeal in the hospital. I can't hate her. But I don't have to like her either.

And why didn't I dress up a bit more? Always in my jeans and tank top as if I fear being stranded on an island again with nothing but a designer swimsuit.

For the record, I am afraid of that happening. Which is why I wear jeans, tank tops, and sneakers almost every time I go out on the island.

When I first arrived, I was a diva. Now, I'm practical and ready for anything. Live and learn.

Keston returns with a special drink for Tabitha. "No sugar," he says. It looks like a glass of water to me. She slides her red lips around the straw like she's a porn star.

Keston reaches behind his back and squeezes my knee. My

heart somersaults. I'm on edge for no reason. But I want to know why these two beautiful people ended their relationship.

They match up so well. They're the same age. They've known each other forever. They are both tall and gorgeous. They share a culture. Most of the time, I don't understand what they're saying to each other when they speak in their dialect.

What do Kes and I have in common?

Other than a great sex life? Nothing! Not our culture, history, age bracket, or looks. I'm not ugly, but I'm no goddess like Tabitha.

Keston spins around as if he can read my thoughts. He's probably going to say something reassuring to me. Let me know that despite our differences, I am deep in his heart, and nothing can break us up.

"Babe," he says, staring into my eyes.

"Yes?" I murmur, ready for a goofy declaration of his love.

"Can you move a little bit over, please? I need to get more club soda from the cupboard behind you."

Tabitha guffaws.

My face grows hot with shame at my less-than-humble attitude.

I jump down from the stool and hustle out of the way so Keston and Dex can grab what they need to keep the drinks flowing.

With no drink in hand, no seat near Keston, and no friend to talk to, I head down to the beach area. Groups of friends and family occupy all the lounge chairs and cabanas.

I don't know any of the hotel guests. And the islanders are all by the bar area.

I wander down to the water's edge. Slip off my brand new, pale pink Vans and roll up the bottom of my jeans. I enter the shallow water, where baby waves roll across my insteps. The sea is warm and leaves bubbles of foam on my toes.

With a thousand stars sprinkled across the sky and a half-moon shining a path of light across the dark sea, I feel like I'm the only person in the world.

Don't feel sorry for yourself, CJ. This is his job. He's busy. You need to find something to do here so you can meet people. Make friends. Get a life.

The last time I made any friends was at college. My friend group of five has stuck together for over twenty years. I don't even know where to start to make new friends.

At that moment, a splash of water made me jump back out of the waves. A school of silvery fish leap into the air together and dive back into the sea, all in sync.

There must be a large fish chasing them for its supper. Keston explained this to me on No Man's Land the first day we were stuck there.

"It's a fish-eat-fish world out here," I say aloud.

"Tell me about it," a voice slurs in the shadows.

I scream and grab my Vans from the sand ready to run back to the bar.

"Don't be afraid. I'm Kelley Kips' brother."

"What the hell?" I bark. "No, you're not. Don't come any closer."

The man in the shadows emerges slowly, the scent of overproof rum leaking from his pores.

"Don't come any closer," I say again, this time with menace. My pink Vans are the only thing I can use to protect myself. I'll throw them if I must.

"I have a secret," the voice slurs.

He steps completely out of the shadows. I gasp. The man standing before me, swaying like a coconut tree in a strong breeze, is the spitting image of my Keston. Tall, handsome, muscles upon muscles.

Except for one thing.

He doesn't have dark skin. He's a very light-skinned, mixed-race man, emphasis on the light-skin.

I know the St. Nicholas islanders are mixed-race people, but how can he be Keston's brother?

My heart crashes into my chest. Is this a joke? Am I being punked?

"I have a secret. About the diary," the man who looks like Keston, but for his skin color, says.

I feel the sand coming up to greet me. I've had too much to drink. Or I'm going crazy.

Chapter Twenty-Seven

Wiry arms grip me before I hit the sand. The smell of rum is so strong, just standing next to this Keston look-alike is making my head spin. As if it wasn't spinning enough already.

"Get off me," I say ungratefully, and push him away.

He lets go of my arm. I collapse on the sand. My throat feels tight. I can't catch my breath. I inhale gulps of air but end up coughing it back out.

"Oh God, I feel ill." I clutch my head and squeeze my eyes shut. Let him be gone when I open them back up.

The man says in a husky voice, "I'm sorry. I didn't take you for a delicate flower."

For some reason, that makes me way more angry than it should.

"Well, who asked you? Oh, wait, nobody! Because you don't exist. You're in my imagination. You're not even the right color to be Keston's brother."

"That would be politically incorrect to say in your country."

"In any country," I agree. "But I said what I said."

The man chuckles. "I see why my brother likes you."

I suck my teeth. "You see nothing. Because you don't exist. If Keston had a brother, he'd have told me."

"I'm the black sheep of the family."

"More like the white one."

He laughs. Unscrews something from his hip. He bends down and passes me a flask. "Take a sip. You'll feel better."

I hold the flask up to the moonlight. I blink twice. The tarnished silver flask has an intricate crest adorning it. Just like the one on the chests at Keston's house.

"Where'd you get this flask?"

"My father."

"Liar."

"Take a sip. I can't believe how rude you are."

That makes two of us.

The man squats on his haunches on the sand. Eye-level with me, he looks even more like Keston with the same strong chin, juicy lips, and sharp cheekbones.

His wavy brownish hair ruffles in the sea breeze. Under the

light of the stars and moon, his eyes look grey. Maybe green. A color that is not brown like Keston's.

I drop my head in my hands. "I thought I knew him."

The flask appears under my nose. God, does this man need a drinking buddy or what?

"Fine!" I say recklessly before grabbing it and taking a huge slug. A flowery liquor slides down my throat. Not that I've tasted many flowers. Or *any* flowers. But this is the only way I can describe the drink.

It makes my eyes sting and my nose run. But it's delicious. I swipe a hand across my eyes.

"What the hell is this?"

"Homemade wine."

"The only wine I've ever drunk is made from grapes. This is not from grapes. What exactly did you make this homemade wine from?"

He takes a sip of the flask. "Dandelions."

"Dandelions?"

"Yup. Dandelion petals and grapefruit."

"What do you call it? Dandelion wine?" I don't expect an answer.

"Yes."

"Nobody makes wine from *dandelions*. They're weeds."

"Haven't you read Ray Bradbury? He's a famous American writer."

I frown. "No. I read romances."

"You should read Ray."

"Does he make dandelion wine, too?" I scoff.

"As a matter of fact, he did."

"You're very strange." If not well-read.

I push myself off the ground with both hands even though he's offering me one of his own.

Face to face with Keston's brother, I see this brother has a small, wicked-looking scar on his left cheekbone. And another Frankenstein scar over an eyebrow.

Where Keston is clean-shaven, this brother has a days-old scruff on his face. A hoop earring hangs from his right ear, and his arms are tatted.

"You look nothing like my Keston," I say. Even though he definitely does.

"Thank God for that," he smiles. "Why are you by yourself on the beach at night anyway?"

I recoil at his accusatory tone as if Keston would ever let anything happen to me.

"What do you want from me?"

"I don't want anything from you. I want to share something with you."

I tilt my head. "Like what?"

"You're not a very trusting person, are you?" he asks, his eyes innocent as if he has no idea how sexy he is.

"Trusting? Ha! Some man shows up out of nowhere . . . ."

"My name is Kelley Kips."

"And claims to be Keston's brother and offers me information about a secret diary that I know nothing about, and I'm supposed to be okay with all that?"

He squints again. "You know about the diary."

"This conversation is done." I head back to the beach bar. I can still hear the music streaming from the speakers. The cocktail scoring game must be running its course by now.

"Here, take this." He shoves the flask into my hand.

I hand it back. "I don't want it."

He tilts his head. A shock of unruly hair falls over one eye. "Why do you think he hasn't told you he has a brother?"

That stops me cold. My heart feels like it's being buried alive. "I don't know," I whisper honestly. "I wish I did."

"Don't be hard on him. He's had a tough life."

"And you haven't?"

He smiles. The same smile I saw in my dreams. Keston's smile. But different.

Oh shit! *This is the man from my dreams.*

"Open your hand."

He doesn't ask any questions. He opens both hands at his sides.

"Oh," I breathe. "I thought you'd have gold coins in them."

His smile hits me like a ray of sunlight in the night. "I don't believe in money."

"Not funny."

"I don't joke about that. Money has torn families apart."

I wonder if he's thinking of any particular family.

"I have to go." I need to go is more like it. Part of me is wondering if I'm asleep and dreaming all this. I pinch my arm hard.

"Ouch!"

"What're you doing?"

"Pinching myself."

"I don't usually have that effect on women. I leave that for Loverboy."

Loverboy was Keston's nickname before he met me.

"What's *your* nickname?" I ask. "Everyone on this island seems to have an alias.

"I never got a nickname."

I frown. That sounds so sad, given how friendly the nickname calling is here.

"I'll call you, . . . '*Thunder*.'"

A burst of laughter escapes his mouth. "Why?"

"Because you were a surprise. And scary. And . . . you look like you could cause a lot of noise."

"You're not incorrect on the last part. I caused a lot of noise many years ago." He sips from his flask and stares dismally out to sea.

"Anyway, I want you to know there are two diaries. You shoud read them togeehter."

"How do you know I found a diary?" I slap a hand over my mouth.

I'd make a terrible secret agent.

"Damn."

"Instincts. You're Keston's girlfriend. You're staying at his house. And you seem curious and smart."

"Really?" I'm ridiculously flattered.

He laughs. "No, I overheard you talking to Keston near the bar. I was in the shadows."

"Stalking us?"

He shakes his head. "Just hanging out. By myself."

I narrow my eyes at him. "Sounds like stalking."

He shrugs. "I like to keep an eye on my little brother."

He squeezes down one eyelid. "I have the other diary. Our grandmother Viola Kips knew what she was doing when she separated the family archives."

"What was she doing?"

"Trying to make sure her grandsons didn't go after the treasure. She lost her beloved son, our father, to the treasure hunt. She didn't want to lose us too."

"You said there are two diaries?"

"Yes. I will lend mine to you if you're interested. After all these years, someone should put them back together. I think they want to be joined. I'm not interested in the treasure. But I want to know the whole story."

I stare at this impossibly handsome man. Even with his scruffy face, unkempt locks, slurring voice, and slouchy linen pants, he's still the most attractive man I've ever seen.

"I'm interested . . . in the diary, I mean."

He grins. Under the starlight, he also looks like the most dangerous man I've ever seen in person.

I shiver. I don't want to know him. But it looks like I may have to.

Chapter Twenty-Eight

After finding my way back to the bar, I tell Keston I'm going to sleep in the villa tonight. He looks disappointed but says okay and holds me close. Normally, I would melt into his embrace.

"Are you almost done here?" I ask to avoid the romantic intimacy.

"Yes," he says, eyes twinkling. "I got all the intel I need for my project."

"That's great." I don't ask about the project. He's already told me it's a surprise. Not that I need any more surprises on St. Nicholas.

The crowd has mostly dispersed. Only some locals remain at the bar and surrounding tables. I see Tabitha at one of the tables talking to women who are sipping glasses of wine.

Is she waiting on him? Are there secrets about Tabitha he's keeping from me the way he's hiding his brother?

I asked him once if he had any family on the island. He said jokingly that everyone was related in some fashion, so they were *all* his family.

When I'd pushed further and asked about his immediate family, he said his mother and sister left to go start over in England after his father died. He was fourteen and remained on the island with his grandmother Viola.

But now I know that's a lie. His brother also stayed.

"Everything okay, baby?"

I cringe inside. Why did he lie? I'm dying to ask him. I shift my eyes to the far corner of the bar. I don't want to lie too.

"I'm tired," I say. "Long day."

"Okay, I understand. I'll see you tomorrow."

"Yes, sure. I left some boxes on your deck. I started going through the historical papers. Can you put them in the living room for me? I'll continue tomorrow." I can hear the stiffness in my tone. As if we are nothing more than acquaintances.

"Sure." He tilts my face toward him so he can look into my eyes.

I give a small smile. A smile as stiff as my voice. I hate this feeling. I want to be happy. I want to feel that joy in my heart from an hour ago, when I was perched on the bar stool behind

Keston as he slung drinks, kissed me, and made me feel like the most special woman in the world.

How can a relationship go from being on top of the world to being turned inside out in the blink of an eye?

"I'll see you tomorrow," I whisper.

Lying in the gigantic bed, downy covers pulled up to my chin, the a/c on full blast, I stare at the ceiling. Tears slide down my cheeks. Damn him! He's supposed to be the one. I thought I found my forever man. The one I'd build a family with.

But the truth is, as much as I love Keston, I've been feeling as if something is a bit off. Which is why I've been needing the villa. For my so-called "mental space."

And why I haven't been ready to move in with him. Maybe even why I complain about wanting more stuff than what he already has to offer, like my own room.

If you truly love someone with all your heart, do you hesitate the way I've been doing? Or do you plunge in with no thought for tomorrow?

But I do love him, I argue with myself.

I love him so much. I close my eyes and remember how Keston looked after me on No Man's Land. Our long conversations and near-death experiences. Our history is short but packed with heartfelt events.

Some quite traumatic.

Can a relationship built on trauma survive? I will Google it tomorrow. Tonight, I want to sleep.

But sleep eludes me. My mind is a whirl of doubts. Now

that I've learned Keston has a secret brother, what do I do about it? Nobody hides a brother.

My subconscious whispers, "But you hid your birth child for almost twenty years. And when you did tell your best friends and your mother, you hoped they'd understand. And lucky for you, they did."

Shush!

Here's the thing about your subconscious, it never shushes.

Chapter Twenty-Nine

I wake up feeling refreshed and as if everything to do with Keston's brother was a dream. I must have hallucinated meeting him. He was too cute to be true. Nobody is that gorgeous in real life.

And no one else saw Kelley Kips.

No one else has ever mentioned that Keston has a brother.

CJ, you have lost your marbles. I laugh out loud. You fell asleep on the beach. That's what happened. You dreamt that crazy nonsense and now you're back safe and sound in your villa.

All the talk and search for pirate treasure had me imagining things. No more Frosty Mermaids for you, woman. I scold myself.

But then I pick up the jeans I'd left on the floor of the closet and something heavy falls out of the back pocket.

Fear tunnels through my heart when I pick up the silver flask with the family crest. Kelley Kips' flask of dandelion wine.

I unscrew the top and sniff. Same fruity scent. I take a tiny sip. Same strong flowery taste. I screw it back and hide it at the bottom of my suitcase.

Fuck!

There's no way I can pretend it was a dream now. Kelley Kips is one smart man. He tucked that flask in my back pocket when I was scrambling around on the beach. So, I'd remember him.

I collapse on the bed and fold my legs under me. My heart races double time. The bedside phone rings and I leap up screaming.

I let it ring until it stops. I stare at my suitcase where I've hidden the flask as if it's a ticking bomb.

Charlotte Campbell's diary is wrapped in plastic under my pillow.

Keston's text messages sending love and kisses this morning are left on Read.

On my laptop where I'm Googling relationships built on traumatic events, an email pops up from Mrs. Harris asking me to stop by the museum. Damn, I forgot about the book club.

Last, Kes sends me a selfie of him and Trixie standing on the beach in front of his home. They're both smiling, with Kes's arm slung around her neck. The flowers tangled in her mane hang limply. They both look as if they're waiting for me to return. My little family. I clutch my heart.

But I'm not ready to talk to him. My mind is busy trying to unravel like *five* mysteries at once.

I message Giselle, asking her to round up the posse. Ten minutes later, they're all on a videoconferencing call.

It's a weekday morning, so Giselle is at her middle school, where she's the principal. For our video call, she's inside her car in the parking lot. I giggle when I see a teacher knock on her driver's side window, asking if she's okay.

Giselle nods and waves the teacher away.

"Must be nice to be the boss," I tell her.

"I'm not the boss of anyone here. I'm more like a circus master."

Katana giggles. She's breastfeeding her newborn while her toddler plays on the floor in the background. "No nanny today. We're trying something new."

"What's new about having a nervous breakdown?" Mikah, our fabulous freelance model friend, answers.

Katana sucks her teeth at Mikah. "Some of us can handle the pressure of doing meaningful work."

"I get my titties sucked *all* the time," Mikah retorts.

Katana and Mikah have a relationship based on pure jealousy, which somehow works for them. They want each other's lives, and they're best friends.

"Oh my God, you two. I swear you should be switched like in the movies. Try out each other's lifestyles and shut the hell up." Giselle's principal voice forces them to stand down.

Or maybe it's the fear of an actual switch.

"Okay, what's up?" Lisa asks. "I'm here trying to solve a great mystery of the universe."

We all grow silent. None of us ask her what the mystery is because we usually don't understand any of her words in relation to each other.

Like we know "star" and "telescope" and "celestial" and "pattern," but when she starts stringing them together, we're lost. Which is why she had to marry another astrophysicist.

"That's wonderful, Lisa," I check-in. "Thanks for being on my call."

"What's going on in paradise, girlfriend?" Katana switches the baby to her other nipple while Mikah rolls her eyes.

"Show off," she mutters.

Giselle eyeballs all of us. "Hit it. Lunch period is coming up soon."

I run through everything that's happened during the past twenty-four hours starting with finding Charlotte Campbell's diary from 1803, which hints at the location of the centuries-old hidden pirate treasure.

They ohh and ahh!

"And I believe she definitely was a Scottish noblewoman in love with the Black pirate king, Kipson. She mentions him as her beloved a few times."

"No way!" Mikah shouts. "This is better than *Bridgerton*!"

The others agree, even Katana who is an avid *Bridgerton* fan.

I tell them about Tabitha showing up and flirting with Keston in front of my face at the beach bar, and I wonder if there is something going on there.

"Probably not," Mikah chimes in. "Some people are just flirty types."

"Like you," Katana adds.

I hurry on so they don't start arguing. "And finally, Keston is hiding a secret brother from me. Remember how I asked if he had any family on the island and he insisted he didn't? Well, that's fake news."

All mouths drop open.

Giselle is annoyed. "What's he hiding that for?"

Katana is too preoccupied with placating a toddler who wants a turn at her breast to give her two cents.

Lisa contemplates the ceiling. "How did you find out?"

"Met him last night. On the beach. No one else was around. He appeared out of nowhere."

Lisa frowns. "No one and nothing appears out of nowhere. Evidence of their presence is always there if you know how to look. Maybe he was following you. Or had information that you'd be on the beach."

"Who'd tell him that?" I ask. "Oh wait, he told me there are two diaries. I totally forgot that." I smack my hand on my forehead. "He says he has one and he knows I have the other diary."

"Whoa!" Lisa sits up straight. Usually, our dramas don't require her to use her million-dollar brain. "Why does he have the other one?"

"Is he definitely Keston's brother?" Mikah interrupts, waving a hand in the air. "Because I'd be interested. We could be best friends dating brothers."

"I thought *I* was your best friend," Katana pipes in.

"You're my *other* best friend," Mikah teases.

I bite my bottom lip trying to recall the full conversation with Kelley Kips last night. My brain hurts it's so jumbled with details.

I snap my fingers. "He has the other diary because it was left to him by Viola Kips his grandmother. He said Viola wanted to split up the diaries and the clues to the treasure so her grandsons would not try to find it. It's how her son died. Keston and Kelley's father."

I gulp a sip of cool water from my bottle.

My girlfriends are mulling it over as Katana juggles her kids, Giselle glances at her watch, Lisa stares at the ceiling, and Mikah stretches like a cat.

"Well?" I ask. "I know I sound ridiculous and overly dramatic, but I feel as if everything is connected. My biggest concern is why Keston is lying to me about his brother. I don't know how to deal with that."

The crack in my voice gives me away. I care a lot more about my relationship being true than I do about pirate treasure or ex-girlfriends or secret brothers.

Mikah wants to know what the brother looks like. "He's not as sexy as Keston, huh?"

"Hotter," I say matter-of-factly. "The man is the most handsome of his species I've ever laid eyes on."

"What species is that?" Mikah asks coyly.

I swat her face on the phone. "He's just your type. Tall, lean, rugged, and tatted up."

"Sounds like every heterosexual woman's type to me," Katana wipes her brow.

"And he carries around a flask of his homegrown and hand-made dandelion wine."

Mikah pretends to swoon. "I'm on my way, CJ. You need help."

"I forgot an important part."

Four faces stare at me.

"He looks like Keston but is very light-skinned."

"How light?" asks Mikah

"Like white."

Chapter Thirty-One

Theories are thrown around about the statistical probabilities of having one dark brother and one light-skin one.

"Who cares about his color? The real issue is why Keston kept his brother a secret from CJ?" Giselle counters.

"Thank you," I say, glad to refocus the discussion. "Maybe he doesn't love me . . . or trust me enough," I gulp.

Giselle takes in my teary eyes. "One of us needs to go to St. Nicholas to lend you support."

I perk up. But then droop back down. "I can't ask any of you to leave your life to come hold my hand. I'm being a big baby. You have your school. Katana has her babies. Lisa just got married."

"I'm in between jobs," Mikah says. "I'll take one for the team."

"More like you'll take the whole team," Katana snorts.

"Don't you wish you were me," Mikah smiles.

"I swear the two of you need a time out," Giselle says. "Okay, it's decided. Mikah will go to St. Nicholas."

"Oh my God," Lisa moans. "Mikah and CJ alone on an island with pirates and mysterious brothers."

"I know," sighs Giselle. "A recipe for disaster."

"Let's start to pray now," Katana quips.

"Ha!" Mikah fake laughs.

"Um. Can you bring my Nespresso machine and a bunch of capsules, please?"

"Seriously?" Mikah asks. "Not a GPS tracker, spy camera glasses, or I don't know . . . *handcuffs?*"

"Handcuffs?" I echo.

Katana shakes her head. "Welcome to Mikah's world."

"Oh. Funny. No just my Nespresso machine and a lot of capsules will do. I need to stay on my toes. Caffeine will help. All this healthy coconut water is not doing the job."

"Rub it in," Lisa sighs.

I thank my friends from the bottom of my heart. "I love Keston. But I need to know the truth."

"Why don't you just ask him?" Katana suggests. She has the

most experience with a serious relationship, but her husband is one in a million.

"What do I do? Walk up to him and say, 'Hey, do you have a brother you're hiding from me?'"

"Yes!" They all shout at the same time.

"I'll think about it."

We say our goodbyes with Mikah adding that she'll text me her flight information. "I'm real excited to come hang out with you, CJ. We'll get to the bottom of this, don't worry."

"You might even find some pirate treasure," Katana says, envy heavy in her voice.

"Nothing would be as valuable as those two munchkins you have there," says Mikah, seriously.

Katana gazes at her sleepy son and daughter with love. "Yeah, that's true."

"Love you guys," I shout, as the screen goes dark.

I feel immensely better knowing Mikah is on her way. She's not my no-nonsense best friend, Giselle, but she's no one to fool with.

Mikah's job as a runway model has taken her around the world and she knows people. I'm sure she can handle Kelley Kips *and* Tabitha with no problem.

As for Keston, I have to figure out what to do. He was so happy last night about his project; I don't have the heart to douse that good cheer with accusations about deceit.

One glance at my watch reveals he'll be at the bar soon. Time to get my butt moving.

Chapter Thirty-Two

I slip the diary from my pillowcase to my backpack. "It's probably you everyone wants, Ms. Charlotte Campbell. But they're not getting you."

Not trusting anyone, I take the backpack to the bathroom, where I prop it on the highest shelf while I shower and change.

Deciding what to wear is a little problem. I long to slink out of the villa in one of my cute swimsuits to frolic in the surf and swing in a hammock while sipping a Keston Kips special. I want to be in vacation mode—happy and carefree.

But today is about deciphering the diary.

I trade the swimsuit for a soft pair of cotton shorts, a tank top, and a baseball cap that I jam down on my curls.

I slip my feet into my pink Vans and head out to the golf cart. Inside my backpack are the essentials I need to translate the diary. A magnifying glass I borrowed from the resort's tourist desk. A new notepad and pen I bought at the gift shop. A headlight with extra powerful beams for God knows what. And two more pairs of gloves to wear while handling the hand-cut pages with care.

I may be overreacting. This diary has obviously sat in Viola Kips' possession for a hundred years or more and I can't be the first person to search it for clues about the location of the treasure.

However, based on Keston's memory, these chests and boxes sat in his grandmother's home all his life and were passed straight to him upon her death. Only Viola and Keston had access to them before I came along.

That means if someone wants to get their hands, and eyes on the diary, all they need to do is walk into Keston's house and look for it.

But the islanders don't walk into each other's homes uninvited. And from what I've seen and heard, there is almost no crime here. It's probably hard to get away with anything since everyone knows everyone else, and it's not as if you can steal a car and go anywhere.

But a diary is not a car.

I'll have to tell Keston straightaway that he needs to start locking his front door. I shouldn't have taken it in the first place, but now I am very glad I did. I am also glad I made the photographed copies of the entire journal.

As for the existence of a second diary, if that is true, then I need to understand what's in this one first, so I can ask the right questions about the second one.

For all these reasons, I bypass the beach bar and head straight for one of the opulent cabanas, with its lavish chairs and tables, to sit down and get to work.

As I'm taking the items out of my backpack and lining them up on the table under the cabana's thatched roof, a familiar figure approaches, twirling his wide tray on his fingertips like it's a magical saucer.

"Good to see you again, CJ," says Dex. "What can I bring you? Coffee? Tea? A mimosa or . . . me?"

I raise my eyebrows at the young man. "Excuse me?"

He swipes his hand in the air as if rubbing away the scandalous suggestion. "Sorry." He dips his head. "The manager said I should be more playful and fun with the guests. Like Keston and his cocktail games. I was practicing."

"You be you, Dex. You're wonderful at what you do. Not all of us can be Keston Kips."

"Tell me about it."

"Although if he had a brother, then that brother could be *like* Keston."

An uncomfortable hush descends.

I'm horrible. My attempt to harvest information from innocent Dex is shameful.

"Well?" I cock an eyebrow at him. "No brother?"

Dex's brown eyes dart left and right, anywhere but on me. "I have to go," he whispers.

And that's how I know.

"Please tell Keston I'll come over to the bar soon. I'm doing a little work first."

"Sure thing."

I push aside the stomach-curling idea of confronting Keston about his secret brother and focus on translating the diary.

First, I glance through the cabana's opening to ensure I'm alone. Straight ahead is the startling blue sea rising and falling in a long-crested wave. The sun beams full measure on the yellow-white sand, sending diamond sparks of light flashing into the atmosphere.

The garden I'm in is sheltered by lofty mango trees, their wide-spreading branches ripe with pink and orange fruit waiting to be picked. Keston blended some mangoes into his cocktails last night, and they were delicious.

If I were the poetic type, I'd think all this natural bounty was better than gold and jewels.

But I'm not a poet. I'm a lawyer. I'm Cuba Gooding Jr. in *Jerry McGuire* yelling, "Show me the money!"

I chuckle at my joke.

After putting on the gloves, I turn the dairy pages. I bend my head until my nose almost touches the pages, intent on understanding the fancy script and old-fashioned words.

My eyes scan for entries that mention my beloved, my Kipson, or any word that could mean *treasure*. As I skim, slowing down to read certain sentences, a portrait of young Charlotte Campbell's life in the early 1800s emerges.

This woman knew how to get a point across in the most delicate fashion, so as not to upset the men, like her father, brothers, and suitors twice her age.

I could learn from her. She wrapped her demands and opinions in cushions of flattery and respect.

The fools of the early 1800s thought so little of Charlotte Campbell because she was a woman that they were blinded by whatever nonsense she threw at them.

Like how many times each month was a woman suffering from the "curse?" Five? Seriously Charlotte? All to escape to her bedroom and be left alone.

Serves them right.

On one page, she sets out a letter to her father begging to choose her own husband. It brings tears to my eyes:

Dearest Father,

With all due reverence to your wisdom and guidance, it is my humble entreaty that I might be afforded the liberty to seek out a companion of my choosing, one whom my heart regards with genuine affection and esteem. I beseech you to grant me leave to pursue a union born not of obligation but of mutual affection and respect.

Poor Charlotte. Having to beg her father to let her love whoever she chose. I admire her fiery spirit.

I wonder if Charlotte had a view of the wild blue sea as she wrote these passages in her diary.

Or was she facing a garden? Was it hot and sunny or balmy and windswept?

My heart hurts for her as I read aloud her entry for January 1, 1803:

A cannon, its roar slicing through the stillness of midnight, heralded the advent of the year 1803. My heart, brimming with a mixture of joy and trepidation, awaits the arrival of my beloved. He shall not partake in the family's festivities; for I harbor a gnawing fear that upon his coming, I shall be cast aside, forever shunned from the bosom of my family.

One month later February 1st, she writes:

Today, my heart is compelled to confess a truth. I find myself irretrievably entwined in affection for one deemed wholly unsuitable by society. He is my heart's choice. In his gaze, I am understood; in his words, I am uplifted; in his presence, I am whole. Let the world forsake me, let my name be sullied amongst the genteel, but I shall not yield this passion, for it is the essence of my being. Thus, I shall love him, come what may, and in this secret chamber of my diary, I dare to declare it: I am his, and he is mine, until the stars themselves burn away.

I press a hand to my bosom (as I imagine Charlotte did back then, thinking about (her beloved). You were only twenty years old, but you knew your heart better than I know mine now.

What powerful words: *"I am his, and he is mine, until the stars themselves burn away."* Knowing Keston's love for the stars, especially his Lucy star, he'd appreciate these words from his ancestors.

"I'm so sorry you had to suffer like this," I whisper to the ghost of the long-ago girl. She had a large, fiery personality in a small body, effused with longing for a man she could not have.

While I have a man who loves me and no obstacles or barriers to contend with. Except the ones we make ourselves.

Damn it. As soon as he's free and we can go somewhere private, I'm going to speak to Keston. Get to the bottom of this confusion. I will channel Charlotte Campbell's spirit and be strong until the stars burn away.

Chapter Thirty-Three

I flip pages frantically to find out what happened to Charlotte and her beloved. I assume it's the same Kipson.

She mentions meeting him several times where the river meets the sea, and the rocks look like a dragon's mouth, and the trees like its tail.

But nothing about buried treasure again. One entry in March 1803 sends my heart racing. She writes:

I found myself once more at the familiar secluded strand, where the sea whispers secrets to the shore. With the moon as our sole witness, we surrendered to a union of souls, an intimate communion whispered between the sighs of the restless sea. Here, we allowed our hearts to speak in the silence of looks and touches. In these pages, I dare confess what the world must not know—my undying love, profound and unwavering, for him who is both my solace and my ardor.

Oh my! Charlotte and Kipson *were* lovers. What else could this mean?

Her desire and longing for her man are clear even in her flowery words. I wish I could express my feelings for Keston as vividly because what she writes, I feel, too. Keston is the person who is my passion and my comfort.

Society may frown on me being the older woman and him being the much younger man. But like Charlotte, I must try to hold tight to the truth of our love and forget society.

My doubts about our cultural differences seem ridiculous after reading her diary. Charlotte and Kipson's backgrounds and cultural differences were immense. Yet, her love for him was unwavering. How did she do it, I wonder.

And how did Kipson feel about Charlotte? He must have loved her deeply to take the chances he did.

I bite my bottom lip and concentrate on the last few months of 1803. Then I see it. Confirmation of who Kipson indeed was. I jump up from the table and hug the diary close to my chest. It's like meeting the ghost of a legend.

October 20th, 1803

My heart, against the counsel of prudence and propriety, has pledged its allegiance to one who reigns not over lands and titles but over the untamed expanses of the sea—my beloved, the pirate king.

This man whom my soul cherishes, who commands the allegiance of the wind and waves as the pirate king, harbors a secret of his own—a past cloaked in nobility and injustice. He is, by birth, a prince of Africa, spirited away from his homeland in chains. Now, in his eyes, I perceive a spirit as free as the winds that carry his sails. A freedom that was hard won. With chains broken and swords taken. A freedom never to be denied again.

I look around wildly. I want to tell somebody. The myths are true. Keston's ancestor was an enslaved African prince who escaped and became a pirate king. As crazy as the myth is, it's true—at least according to the woman who loved him. My hands shake as I turn the pages to continue reading.

I am fully aware of the dangerous course upon which I have embarked, loving a man marked by both infamy and outlawry. Yet, in the depth of my being, a voice whispers that true love is itself a form of rebellion—a defiance of conventions that would dictate the boundaries of affection and the sanctions of the heart. Thus, I record here, under the silent watch of the stars, my undying love for him—the sovereign of my heart, the pirate king.

I choke up. Tears brim in my eyes, ready to fall.

I can't bear to read anymore. Not right now.

I want to hold on to the idea they were happy and free together in their hidden world. *"True love is itself a form of rebellion."*

If this woman, barely out of her teens, can defy convention, declare her true love, and follow her heart, who are we, well, *who am I*, to hesitate?

It's time I rebel fully. Love deeply. Truly. Madly. Like Charlotte and Kipson.

But first, I must find out why Keston did not tell me about his brother Kelley.

Chapter Thirty-Four

I fire up the golf cart and push it to its max speed of eight miles per hour, twisting and turning around the garden paths lined with squat palm trees, bushes of pink hibiscus, and lizards sunning themselves on top of the solar lights planted in the ground.

Tiny hummingbirds zip about dipping their iridescent

heads to drink nectar from the flowers. They fly by so fast they almost take out my eye.

"Watch it, my friends."

The scent of coconut oil and salt drifts my way.

I feel exhilarated that I get to see my love Keston soon, despite doubts about the whole "I have not told you I have a brother" thing. There must be a good reason why he didn't tell me.

I slide my golf cart to a stop next to the sandy beach bar, like a figure skater at the end of a routine. If I expect a round of applause from Keston, I won't be getting any. His back is to me, and his head is bowed next to Tabitha as they look at a laptop side by side.

The jealousy bug shoots its poison at me. I force shield it away. It's not good to become annoyed every time I run into Tabitha St. Clair.

First, Mikah is on her way. I'll soon have a backup.

Second, I believe that Keston loves me, and I love him, and nothing will get between us until the stars burn away.

Three, I'm a grown-ass woman.

That last reason lacks conviction. So what I'm grown. Ex-girlfriends should not be hanging around their ex-boyfriend's jobs every day.

What would CC do?

That young woman defied *everyone* for her true love. All I have to do is defy this one woman. Emphasis on defy!

Easy peasy.

Tabitha must hear my approach. Or my menacing thoughts about how to defy her.

She glances over her shoulder and locks eyes with me. I see something I don't expect to see. Is that happiness? Admiration? Nah!

That can't be for me.

I look over my own shoulder to see if someone else is behind me, causing those emotions to flicker in Tabitha's eyes.

Walking up in his slouchy manner, grizzled chin catching the orange light of the evening sun, linen pants rolled and tied at the ankles, feet bare, a smoky scent emanating from his bare chest, where abs dip and ripple, making women (and men) stop and drool into their drinks, is none other than Mr. Secret Brother himself.

Kelley Kips is not smiling.

Oh my God!

Why do I feel as if a showdown is coming?

Why isn't Mikah here yet? I glance at my Fitbit. She's arriving first thing tomorrow morning.

I inhale deeply and step off the pathway to make room for the new gunslinger in town.

"Hi there, CJ," he says softly.

I do a little wave from my hip.

Keston spins around. His eyes lock on me first. As if I'm all that matters.

I nod, frozen in place. I see Kes's shoulders square themselves at the sight of Kelley strolling breezily toward the bar.

Tabitha hops off her stool and runs, yes *r u n s*, in high heels, on the sand, to this man.

If I'm not mistaken, she may be in love with this brother too.

Her body language is all *"pick me, pick me."* Is she fawning over him? I cover my mouth with my hand so no one can hear me giggle.

Keston walks over to my side, slides one arm around my waist, and leans over to kiss my lips. It's firm and warm and fast.

But his eyes are deadlocked on Kelley.

I want to ask, "Who's that?" to see what he'd say. But I can't get my tongue to work.

Tension thickens the air.

"What're you doing here?" Keston's deep voice asks as Kelley approaches with Tabitha hanging onto his arm. I'm unsure if she's leading him toward us or trying to drag him away.

Either way, Kelley Kips is his own man. He slouch-strolls like he has all the time in the world. It's quite impressive. It's as if he *invented* swagger. He's not doing anything to exude it. It's all-natural.

"Yo," he says to Keston.

I cringe. I've never heard anyone address Keston with anything except respect, admiration, or friendly banter.

Kelley's tone offers none of that. It's more a matter of fact. Like, "I see you standing there."

I feel Keston's body tense next to mine.

My bottom lip catches between my teeth. I find my hand gripping Keston's, pressing down on the fleshy part of his palm as if to say, "I got your back."

Kelley stops walking in front of me, ignoring Keston.

"She'd have liked you a lot," he says. "Viola, I mean. *And* Charlotte." He tilts his head as if that last part is surprising to him.

Tabitha frowns. "Who's Charlotte?"

Keston pushes me behind him and steps to his brother.

"I said, what do you want?"

"Her," Kelley says calmly. "I want to speak to CJ."

Even though I can't see the expression on his face, Keston's hand loosens in mine, giving me an idea of what he may be feeling.

Betrayed?

Hurt?

Confused?

I wish the sand would sweep me up and bury me in a castle.

I never got a chance to tell Keston that I met Kelley. Now, it looks as if I'm the one keeping a secret from *him*.

What the hell!

"Don't be mad at her," Kelley's voice drops low. "She was alone on the beach. I was checking to make sure she was okay."

Oh God.

Tabitha's eyes narrow into slits. If looks could kill, I'd be dead right now. I'm thankful Keston has not let go of my hand. Otherwise, I might collapse right here.

What would CC do? I ask myself.

A moment of silence passes as everyone stares at each other.

She'd lie to save her true love's feelings. Maybe some lies are okay. I look at them all and say, "I've never met this man before in my life."

Three sets of eyes stare at me. One in disbelief. Another with disdain. And the last, the only one that matters, with deep love and confusion.

When I say deep love, I mean it. Keston's dark brown eyes hold me in their gaze as if I am precious. Like he wants to protect me from everything. Probably from myself too.

His warm embrace surrounds me even when his arms are not touching me.

"Can I talk to you alone, Keston?" I ask.

He nods.

"I'll see you later, Tabitha. Thanks for your help," Keston unties his bar apron.

"What about . . . ," Tabitha starts. She shifts her stance toward Keston, but she doesn't leave Kelley's side.

"Later, we can finish it later." Keston's voice is strained.

Kelley, to his credit, does not confront me about my outrageous lie. The look in his one grey, one green eye is now resigned as if his existence has been denied a lot.

In the fading light, I see his complexion is more olive*ish*. His too-long hair is streaked by the sun, but it's not blond. He could be a surfer, a farmer, a hitchhiker, or the lead singer in a band.

Where Keston is classically handsome and easy on the eyes, Kelley is someone who it's hard to look away from, but you don't know why.

"I have that thing for you, CJ," he says as I turn to leave.

I'm dying to know if it's the other diary. But it'll have to wait.

I murmur something like, "Okay, thanks," and hurry off.

Keston closes out his shift and gives Dex instructions for the rest of the evening.

I sit on a bar stool hugging my arms and legs, feeling guilty as sin. Though I have not done anything wrong.

Dex is unusually quiet, avoiding my eyes. He cheers up

when Keston whispers something to him and claps him on the back.

"Come on troublemaker." Keston throws an arm around my shoulders. In his other hand he's carrying his dry bag and a large machete.

I gulp. "Why do we need that?"

He grunts, "You never know. Do you have what *you* need? I want to take you out."

I don't, but I'm not about to drive the golf cart back to my villa until I've spoken to him.

"Yep," I say.

"Good. I have a surprise for you." His smile is warm and loving. His cheerfulness makes me think I imagined the whole Keston-Kelley encounter.

"Okay, but I need to talk to you."

He grimaces. "I need to talk to you, too. I'm not sure what is going on, but I've already planned out our evening, and I'm not letting him or anything else get in our way of having a good time."

"Okay." Part of me is relieved we aren't discussing it yet. The other part is frustrated that I have to wait.

Instead of heading for the parking lot where he normally parks his motorbike, we traverse the winding stone path to the resort's dock.

The gleaming catamaran that left us behind on No Man's Land six months ago is tied up there. I shudder when I see it.

"Where are we going?"

Keston points to his blue boat tied up behind the resort's big catamaran.

"Isn't it getting late for a boat ride?" I ask.

He helps me in and starts the engine.

"Never. The sea is very calm tonight. I want to show you something."

I settle into the seat next to his, and watch as he leaps out, unties the line, tosses it into the boat and jumps back in. I notice his leg is working beautifully, no hesitation or small jerky movements like before.

"How's your leg feeling?" I ask.

He sticks it out. "See for yourself."

Muscles pop out in his thigh and calf.

I blink. "Looks alright to me."

"You good?" he asks.

I can tell his question isn't about my physical comfort and more about my emotional state.

I'll play along for now. "Yes, I'm good."

"We're going to cruise along the coastline for a bit," he says, steering us out to sea.

When he's past the other boats in the bay, he turns north and zips past bushy green hills, long stretches of golden beaches, a lagoon that opens into the sea, and numerous small outcroppings.

These rocky patches of land look like they broke off from the mainland ages ago.

"I have to keep my eyes open to see if any new rocks have emerged since the last time that I motored up the coast," he says.

"Does that happen often? New formations in the sea, I mean."

"Not really."

He points out waterfalls cascading between the crevices in the cliffs. The sky glows with a deep orange light that reflects on the water.

"This is such a beautiful island," I sigh.

"Like a Garden of Eden," he grins. "That's what it's been called."

I settle back in my seat, eyes on the orange ball of a sun hovering on the horizon between sea and sky.

The air is warm and humid, but the breeze coming off the sea is cooling.

I trail my hand off the side of the boat, enjoying the sea spray.

"That rock in the sea is fairly new." Keston points to a high formation of boulders disconnected from the mainland. One lone tree grows on the very top.

"Looks like a lighthouse tree."

"That's a good name for it," he says. "It has to be sturdy and solid to survive alone like that against high waves and wind."

I snap a photo of the tree with my phone's camera. "It looks lonely."

"This rock has been separated from the mainland for about fifty years. One minute, there was nothing here; the next, there was an earthquake, and the mountain's edge broke off and drifted to this spot. You can squint and see how the pieces used to line up."

I squint as Keston slows down the boat. "Yes," I shout. "It's like a jigsaw puzzle."

"My Dad used to bring me out here fishing. He told me about this rock and showed me how it once connected to the island."

My ears perk up. Is he telling me about his father as a transition to talking about Kelley?

"What else did he show you?"

Keston flings his arm out. "Everything. We spent a lot of time cruising up and down this coast. I know every inlet, every bay, probably where every bird nest is located too."

I laugh. "Sounds like you guys were close."

His face shuts down. "Yeah."

I have so many questions, but with the engine's noise, I

don't want to miss anything he says. I'll hold my questions for the time being.

I'm just going to sit here and admire Keston as he navigates our boat through the highs and lows of the dark blue waves— kind of like how he steadfastly navigates our new life together.

Every once in a while, he turns to me with a loving smile. Far be it for me to ruin this moment.

Night has descended quickly, as it does here, but the sky is aflame with stars. We float alone on the serene sea, the quiet hush of the night wrapping around us like a secret.

Keston steers the boat toward the entrance of what appears to be a mangrove lagoon and turns off the engine. The silence is broken by the gentle lapping of small wavelets against the boat.

Giant mangroves grow thick branches overarching each other alongside the edges of the lagoon. Their branches look like ghost arms under the half-moon's light.

If anyone needed the perfect hideout, this would be it. Was this what it was like when CC and Kipson met late at night on the island? Only the moon and stars observing their love?

"Watch," Keston murmurs. He reaches out, skimming his hand across the water's surface, and suddenly, the sea comes alive with light. Brilliant blue swirls erupt around us, bathing the boat in a surreal, glowing aura.

"What *is* this?" I ask fascinated.

"Bioluminescence," he says proudly as if he created this natural phenomenon.

His smile widens as he swoops up the water to reveal the sparkling light of millions of algae or whatever produces bioluminescence.

With each movement he makes with his hand, bursts of blue blossom.

"I feel as if we're floating on the cosmos." My laughter spills into the night, and I cover my mouth with both hands. "I can't believe it. Like a dream."

He pulls my hands away and holds them in his. "This is your surprise, baby. Laugh as loudly as you want."

Wrapping both his arms around me from behind, he leans me gently over the edge of the boat.

"Touch it."

I sweep my hand across the surface of the water. Blue-green light dances along the surface.

"I'm making magic?" I whisper.

"You are the magic," he says. Then he kisses the back of my head with such tenderness that tears form in my eyes. Not because I'm sad—the opposite. I have never been happier in my life.

"The bioluminescence is the mysterious, shining life of the ocean," he says. "Just the way stars are the mysterious, shining life of the sky."

I turn in his arms. His eyes meet mine, lit by the ethereal blue around us.

"Thank you," I whisper. "For showing me this."

Was this how it was for Charlotte and Kipson, I wonder? Did they find a world of beauty beyond their restricted, narrow, and dangerous ones? Where true love shone like this biolumi-nescence.

I wave my hand across the water once more just to see it turn bright blue. Keston uses a paddle and propels us through the lagoon leaving a wake of azure light shimmering on the surface.

"It's like an alien being," I say, trying to scoop some up and failing. The blue glow slips through my fingers with the water.

"I want to catch it." I stick both hands in the water this time.

Keston's throaty laugh in the silence of the night reminds me of when we were stranded on the island and had only each other for company. I grew to love him there. I love him even more now.

I give up my quest to capture the bioluminescence and snuggle up next to him.

He nuzzles my neck with his nose because his hands are busy paddling us around the lagoon.

"Anytime, baby. I hope I can always show you magic in the world."

I slip my arms around his neck and rest my head on his shoulder.

In the middle of this dazzling ballet, the boundaries between us dissolve.

"My Keston," I whisper.

"My CJ," he whispers back. He drops the paddle in the boat and scoops me up in his arms. I wrap both legs around his waist as he slides onto the long bench at the front of the boat.

His lips find mine. We kiss like we've never kissed before. As if we're sealing our hearts and souls together.

"Do you promise to love me forever?" he asks, his eyes full of the starlight shining from above.

I nod my head. "As long as the moon rises, the stars shine, and the bioluminescence glows."

He laughs. "Woman, you must never leave me."

"Never," I whisper. "Ever."

Chapter Thirty-Seven

We had a beautiful night. First, the boat ride out to the bioluminescent lagoon. Then a hot shower together at Keston's house followed by sweet love on the kitchen table.

I'd mentioned that I'd always wanted to have sex on a kitchen table, so he'd obliged.

Although I got most of the loving. Kes laid me down on the table, pulled up a chair, spread my legs, and ate my pussy until I was limp and crying for him to stop.

"But I'm just getting started baby," he'd smirked. "You know what they say?"

"What?" I panted as his tongue stroked my sore and aching pussy. He raised up his head and winked, "If you can't stand the heat, get out of the kitchen."

"Okay, let's go. Please."

"Thought so." He picked me up and carried me to the bedroom.

"Finally, we're going to make love like normal people," I said.

But there was nothing normal about the way he ripped off my towel and made me stand up on the bed facing him while he sat with his back leaning against the headboard.

I spread my legs for balance.

Which I guess was the point.

My fingers gripped the headboard as he kissed my pussy, talking to it, asking my pussy if it wanted to be licked, sucked, or stroked.

I giggled.

"Or maybe you want this, huh?"

He rubbed his nose in a slow agonizing circle on my clit.

I groaned out loud. "I love that."

He nosed it up and down, side to side and in circles, creating the most delicious friction, sending waves of excitement through my body.

I felt a finger probing at the entrance of my streaming wet vagina. I arched my back. He dove the finger into my throbbing pussy and pumped it gently in and out to match the rhythm of his nose.

"You're kinky." I laughed throatily.

"Not yet."

I glanced down to see what his hands, fingers, and nose were doing. Sensations ripped through me everywhere.

His cock was engorged beneath me, standing erect and ready.

"What are you doing?" I cried.

"Making sure this sweet thing is ready to take all of me."

He slid a second finger inside me. "I don't know if two fingers are enough," he said, mock sadly.

He stopped talking and kissed my clit.

I grabbed his hair and held it against my pussy. "More," I breathed. "I want more of that."

"You like me to finger fuck you?"

I nodded, unable to speak.

"And suck you?" He enveloped my clit in his mouth, taking turns teasing it with the side of his tongue and sucking it with his whole mouth.

I felt like I'd died and gone to heaven. The combination of his fingers gliding in and out of my vagina made me overflow with a well of excitement.

When I thought I couldn't take anymore, he turned me around and bent me over. My ass stuck up right in front of his face.

"Oh my God!" I shrieked as he licked the rim of my ass. My toes curled. My ass shook and shivered under his tongue.

Knowing Kes, that was only the beginning.

He rimmed it, licked it, and then unexpectedly slid a wet finger in, teasing the opening until I felt it blossom under his tongue and finger.

With two digits still finger fucking my pussy hole, he licked my asshole. I quivered and shook all over.

"I'm coming," I shouted for the whole world to hear.

I have heard about it but never experienced the squirt thing. But there is no other way to describe it. My pussy squirted its cum all over the towels, the sheets, his legs, my feet.

It was a glorious, messy affair. And I would not want it any other way.

That man made magic on and in every part of me.

After I came, screaming the whole time, he turned me around and slid me down on his big, fat cock.

For the first time, I took all eight or nine inches easily. It felt so good filling me up.

I held onto the headboard, gripped his hair, and squeezed his shoulders.

I rode that sweet dick as if I were riding to win a race.

I squealed and yelped at each thrust of his hardness. He held my hips and slid me down hard over and over again until I thought I would faint or stop breathing.

The headboard banged against the wall with each thrust.

My head thrashed about, my eyes glazed over, and my lungs sang for mercy. It was a wild wild ride.

Finally, he, too, was panting and shouting my name.

I covered him with kisses until we collapsed together in the messy bed.

Neither of us spoke for a good five minutes.

When my breathing steadied, I glanced over at my man. He winked and said, "Welcome to the dark side."

I smacked his arm. "Very funny."

We took another hot shower and started over with a lubricating lotion this time.

By the time we stopped finding new ways to make each other explode with rapture, the moon had disappeared, and the day was softly breaking.

"I can't believe we made love all night."

"Believe it, baby. I'm going to put a small fridge in the bedroom so we never have to get out of bed."

I laughed merrily. My inner voice was saying, "You ain't never going back to New York, bitch."

"What's so funny?" he asked.

"Oh, nothing," I said. "Just nothing at all."

Chapter Thirty-Eight

"I do not have a brother," Keston says angrily. "Who told you that lie?"

I stare at him, utterly incredulous. "Seriously?"

Keston scoffs. "Probably that maniac who showed up at my job. He's delusional. There is no proof we're related. I don't even know that guy. Never spoke to him before."

I walk away from Keston. We're getting nowhere. What's most disturbing is not his outright denial of having a brother, but his insistence that he doesn't know Kelley.

"You do know him," I assert, my voice firm. "You said everyone here knows each other."

"I was wrong."

"You're being obtuse."

"I don't know what that means. And how can we go from making love to this ridiculous argument? Why are you letting this man come between us?"

I roll my eyes. In one sense, he's correct; Kelley is coming between us.

I sit on the porch swing and rock myself back and forth with my foot on the floor.

We'd caught a couple of hours of sleep and were up early because soon we'd have to go pick up Mikah from the airport.

Trixie is asleep on the porch, which is where we found her when we arrived back at Keston's dock last night.

Poor baby must have slept during the intense lovemaking.

It appears she can sleep through anything. Her snores and occasional farts are the only sound she makes as Kes and I argue.

"Here." Keston bangs his way out the front door and hands me a mug.

I accept the warm cup. "Thanks?"

"It's tea."

He's shirtless and shoeless and sexy as hell, leaning one arm high against the doorframe, his ankles crossed, mug in his hand.

I don't know if the tea is a peace offering or if he's calling a truce. I sip mine quietly, trying to regroup.

I need to get to the bottom of this confusion. And I need to do so before Mikah arrives. I can't have her showing up and me saying, "Oops, he didn't lie. It's my bad."

"So let me ask you this . . . have you ever seen Kelley Kips before?"

"Don't call him that."

"What, Kelley?"

"No, Kips. He's not my brother. His last name is Harris."

I frown. "Like Mrs. Harris?"

"Yup. That's his mama."

"Whoa? Are you kidding me?"

He shakes his head as he sips his tea. "Nope."

I lean back in the porch swing, my foot pushing fast and furious against the floorboards. I'm swinging so hard that the back of the swing is hitting the porch wall.

"You're making me dizzy, woman,"

"Oh, sorry." I tuck my foot under me.

"You've got some crazy connections on this island."

He shrugs. "I told you; we're all related."

"Right, except for you and Kelley, it seems." I didn't mean it to come out snarky, but it does.

He frowns at me.

I scowl at my man, which is hard to do given how hot he looks in his bad-boy lean.

"Why'd you ask him what he was doing at the Cocoa Reef Resort?" I ask.

"Why'd he say he wants to talk to you?"

"You're answering a question with a question."

"And you're not answering *my* question."

"It's about the diary in your grandmother's chest. Kelley knows something about it."

He stares at me. "I'll kill him if I have to."

My mouth drops open. "You didn't just say that."

"I did. I would. I will."

"Keston Kips!" I stand up, shocked. "You sound like a . . . like a . . . I can't even think of a word."

"Like a *pirate*? It must run in my genes," he says snidely.

I slam my fists on my hips. "I'm not going to be with a man who talks like this."

"You promised you'd stay with me forever last night. I guess forever comes mighty fast in your world."

"Arrrgh! Are we having our first fight?" I ask, stomping across the porch. This time, poor Trixie leaps up and dashes off into the yard.

"Look what you did. You scared our donkey."

"Her name is Trixie."

"No, it's not. It's Starlight."

"Since when?"

"Since two nights ago when I arrived home alone. Starlight was here looking at the stars with me."

"Oh."

"Hee-haw," the donkey brays from across the yard as if confirming his story.

"I like Trixie," I say softly.

"Fine," he sighs. "We can call her Trixie Starlight."

"Trixie Starlight Kips," I suggest.

The donkey brays louder this time.

Both of us chuckle, then stop.

"I can't believe you'd kill a man just because he wants to speak to me."

"That's not the only reason. It's on account of him that my dad died, and my mother and sister moved away. He's why I lost my entire family."

"What?"

Keston slumps onto the porch swing. I sit beside him, taking his hands in mine. "Do you want to talk about it?"

He shakes his head.

"Okay, so you don't know Kelley. But he ruined your life?"

Keston wraps an arm around me and pulls me onto his lap.

"Yes. And if he tries to take you away, I'll kill him. I promise."

Chapter Thirty-Nine

Keston's friend Alex arrives to drive us to the airport to collect Mikah.

Keston and I are speaking to each other in a cordial manner, but I'm still upset he denies he has a brother.

That's plain childish.

It's clear Kelley is related to him somehow. But seeing as

how difficult it is for Keston to talk about, I've decided to let it slide for now.

"To be continued," I'd told him.

To which he'd grunted, "Maybe."

Alex and Keston discuss the latest island news and everything from fishing to golf. They tried to bring me into the conversation, but I shook my head and stared out the window, going over all the stuff that had happened in the past week.

For a quiet island, there was a lot of action.

I'm dying to get Alex alone to ask him about Kelley. I don't get my chance until we reach the airport, and Keston stops to chat with one of his old classmates.

"Oh, you met Kelley Harris Kips?" Alex says when I bring it up. "Don't call him Keston's brother. He'll get angry."

"But they have the same last name. They're related, right?"

Alex nods in a noncommittal way.

"What do you know about Kelley?"

Alex scratches his head. "Not a lot. He didn't go to school with us. He's . . . I don't know how Americans say it . . . umm, like he's special."

"He's special?"

"Here, we say he's a bit off." Alex touches his head and spins a finger in a circle.

I smack down his hand. "That's not nice."

"He's smart. He's just not normal. I don't know what you call that."

"I think you're saying Kelley is on the spectrum."

"Yeah, that's it. He's special."

I mull that over. That could explain the slightly off-kilter way he has of moving and speaking. Or that could be his unique personality.

And then the way he ignored Keston and focused on me. Like he had tunnel vision.

But regardless of whether Kelley Harris Kips is on the spectrum, he has something to give me, and I bet it's the other diary.

"Are they related?" I ask again. "It seems as if they must be. Kelley told me he and Keston are brothers."

I don't mention that Kelley has no reason to lie to me.

Alex hoots. "You better ask Keston. It's his story to tell."

"Shoot. He doesn't want to talk about it."

"I don't want to talk about what?" asks Keston, hugging me from behind.

At that moment, Mikah emerges from the glass doors, her long legs striking in a hot pink mini dress.

I hurry over to her.

"Where in the world do you think you're going?" I hug my friend tightly.

"I just came from a party, dearie. No sleep for the wicked."

"Thank you for coming." I hug her again to make sure she's here.

"Oh, praise the Lord. There is a heaven." Alex swoons in front of Mikah. "Welcome to St. Nicholas."

While Mikah is getting a proper St. Nicholas Island greeting from Alex, which includes a cold beer at nine o'clock in the morning, Keston greets Mikah with a hug and a kiss on her cheek.

"I feel as if I already know you," he says.

"Same," she says.

A smile grows on his handsome face.

I look at him as if I'm Mikah meeting him for the first time. I would be swooning for sure.

"So, you're going to be my future brother-in-law," Mikah teases.

Keston does not hesitate. "I am."

I blush.

Alex clears his throat. "And I'm available to drive you anywhere you wish to go for as long as you're here."

I raise my eyebrows at Keston. "That's news to me."

"Go with it," he laughs. He tries to grab Mikah's carry-on bag, but Alex gets to it first.

"Thank you, Alex," Mikah purrs. "Boy, they make them big and brawny here." She squeezes one of Alex's biceps. His eyes bug out.

"Yes, ma'am."

I forgot how it is with Mikah. She gets all the attention. The rest of us follow in her wake.

Keston smacks my butt as we walk to the car. "How am I doing?"

I laugh. "I think you passed."

After dropping us off at my villa, Keston is ready to head to the beach bar for his shift.

Alex, who is an a/c man with his own business, offers to hang around.

Keston peels him away. "Let the women catch up."

I mouth "thank you" to Keston.

When we're finally alone, Mikah fans herself with her hand. "Wooza, CJ. That man is a beast."

I frown. "What?"

"Your man, Keston. Body for days! Charm to boot. And you said he's smart, too. I've been looking for a man like him for a long time. No wonder his ex is still hanging around."

"Thanks?"

She bats very long fake eyelashes at me. "Good thing we're besties."

"Good thing," I agree. For sure I wouldn't stand a chance if Mikah decided to go after Keston. She pulls men with her looks alone. Add her flirtatious attitude. Game over.

After strolling around the villa, ordering room service, and popping open a bottle of bubbly, Mikah yawns and says, "Okay, bring me up to date. I want the facts only. No commentary. Start with what you know for sure."

Mikah's long legs are propped up on the sofa. Her long hair is pulled back in a loose, messy bun.

As soon as the men left, she showered and changed from her hot pink mini to her "casual" wear: an all-in-one short body suit that hugs her every dip and curve and gold strappy sandals.

For most people, the ensemble would scream "trying too hard." For Mikah, it's more like "*I'm not trying at all.*"

I stare at my friend. "Who taught you to talk like a . . . secret agent?"

She laughs languidly. "No, darling. It's what I tell all the designers when I show up for a shoot or a call. People like to waste time. I don't."

"You got us all fooled, Mik."

"I know. It's what I do."

"Remember when you told us that you were majoring in marine biology so you could wear a swimsuit to work?" I sip my glass of bubbly.

It's barely ten o'clock in the morning, but I'm feeling relaxed and even festive now that I have one of my loyal wing-women by my side.

Mikah laughs. "And you all believed me!"

"And now you *do* get to wear a swimsuit to work."

She screws up her nose. "But I have my degree."

"That you do." We click glasses together. "Here's to college life."

"Here's to finding true love," Mikah says seriously. "I want some of what you got."

"It's not all rainbow and butterflies," I remark, remembering my and Keston's blowout this morning. "Sometimes you have to . . . umm."

"Beat their ass?"

"What?" I spit out champagne on the white sofa and instantly mop it up with the edge of my t-shirt. "Mikah!"

Just saying, "Got to keep 'em in line, right?"

"Lord alone knows the kind of men you date."

She pouts. "That's the problem. I don't date. Hardly ever."

"What are you talking about? You're always with a new guy."

"Emphasis on '*new*.' I'd like to find a keeper." She sighs.

I study my drop-dead gorgeous friend. Because her comments are so outlandish, we usually ignore Mikah's laments about men, dating, and romance.

But now, I wonder if her pretend jealousy at Katana's married-with-children-lifestyle is real—something to consider.

The morning whirls between drinks, room service salads, and me relaying all the important information, sticking to the facts.

When I'm done, Mikah tells me to try on some of her clothing. She unzips her carry-on, and brightly colored silky fabrics burst out.

Shimmering greens and misty pinks. Startling fuchsia and dreamy blues.

"Wow! You brought so many clothes. Did you remember my Nespresso machine?"

She flicks a long finger at her shoulder bag. "I managed to squeeze it in there.

Lighter than I thought.”

“Thank you so much.” I dive for her bag and extract my precious machine. I’m ready to hook it up and start getting highly caffeinated.

Mikah stops me. “All the clothes are for you. You’ve been looking like a hobbit lately.”

I glare. “Jeans and a tank top and sneakers are not hobbit clothes. They are good and practical. Besides, I have a sundress . . . but a donkey wears it.”

Mikah doesn’t bat an eyelash. Instead, her tone softens. “You won’t get stranded on an island again, CJ. You can wear a cute sundress or a sexy beach outfit once in a while.”

My body tenses up at the idea of trading my safe clothing for impractical ones. “Maybe later,” I say.

“Maybe now!” Mikah throws me an outfit. “Go change.”

When I’m done, Mikah claps. “Look at you all *Pretty Woman*ish!”

I spin around in front of the full-length mirror. The light rose-colored vintage sundress with a floaty skirt and a boat-neck collar is darling—it’s like what I used to wear.

My legs feel tingly happy, like I’ve freed them from a denim prison.

“Okay,” I grouse. “I’ll wear it.”

Part of me is excited to see what Keston thinks. It’s crazy how traumatic events can change you to your core. Even the way you dress. Maybe wearing clothes that I used to love is one way to practice healing.

I do a quick twirl before sliding into the golf cart.

“CJ is back.” My subconscious whispers. I roll my eyes for no other reason than it can’t object.

“Give me the grand tour of your beautiful St. Nicholas,” Mikah says, sliding in beside me. She props her feet on the golf cart’s console and drops her dark sunglasses over her eyes. My inadequacy pops up like a whack-a-mole.

Even in my pretty dress, I feel like a chauffeur driving a movie star. Some feelings can't be remedied by new clothes.

"Well, over here is the garden. And over there is the beach," I say, as I turn the key and the mini engine roars to life.

"Take the slow road," Mikah says, totally missing my sarcasm. "I need to go over the facts."

I chug along, my eyes on the cloudy sky. The sun has been slipping in and out from behind the dark canopy all morning. A storm is brewing on the horizon. The word "storm" scares me, although I try not to show it.

I google the weather report twice daily to stay abreast of sudden changes in the atmosphere—a tornado, a hurricane, a sea witch, anything unusual.

"Let's see," Mikah ticks off her fingers as I stay on the pathway between the manicured bushes and trees.

"You have a man named Kelley who is a loose cannon and who may or may not be Keston's brother or some other relative, and he has something to give you."

"Right."

"You found an old diary that may have belonged to Keston's ancestor. It mentions a buried treasure."

I nod vigorously. "And true love."

"Commentary," Mikah shakes her head.

"No," I argue. "It's a fact."

Mikah taps her sparkly fingernails on the top of the golf cart. "*Irrelevant* fact then."

"Love is never irrelevant," I mutter.

Mikah ignores me. "You also have an anonymous caller who says you have something *she* wants."

I mentioned this to Mikah earlier after completely forgetting to tell Keston yesterday.

The villa's phone had rung a few times, and when I finally answered it, a voice said I had something it wanted. I asked who it was but got no answer.

For some reason, I wasn't nervous about it. I was too caught up in the whole secret brother drama. Also, the voice wasn't threatening—more like stating a fact.

"I don't know if it's a woman."

"It's a woman. A man would tell you he's coming for it."

"Oh, okay." I side-eye Mikah. "Are you sure you're not a spy disguised as a supermodel?"

"If I tell you, I'll have to kill you."

"Fine. I don't want to know."

I think back to Mikah's work trips over the past twenty years. Some in international locations you wouldn't think had fashion shows. Plus, there's her shrewdness. The men she's been with. The times she's disappeared. Her ability to seem like a bimbo while being the sharpest person in a room.

"What did you get your degree in again?" I ask casually.

"We're being followed."

"What?" I slam on the brakes. Not that we were going very fast. One of Mikah's arms shoots out to protect me from hitting the steering wheel.

"You want me to drive chickadee?"

"Sure. Did you say we're being followed?"

She slides over to my seat and presses on the accelerator. "Let's see what this baby can do."

"Not much," I mutter.

Spoken too soon, Mikah somehow gets the cart to reach max speeds of at least fifteen miles per hour. She zooms along the pathways, knocking over a few bushes.

"What're you doing?" I squeal.

"Losing our tail."

"You're joking, right?"

"I don't joke about being followed. It's my biggest pet peeve."

I stare at my glamorous friend in her slinky, all-in-one bodysuit and strappy sandals.

"Who *are* you?"

"Duck."

I duck my head as Mikah drives the golf cart under a low-hanging branch *very* fast.

"Does Katana know about you?" I shout.

"Know what?"

"Your secret occupation as a spy?"

Mikah laughs. "She's the only one who knows I'm an asset. You can say, agent. Leave the word 'secret' out; it's so old movie-ish." She drives the cart along the riverbank's edge that flows to the sea.

I blink. "I was joking."

"I wasn't. Also, we may have to ditch this buggy."

I glance over my shoulder. "I don't see anyone."

At that moment, a loud thud hits the top of our cart. I scream and duck for cover.

Mikah chuckles. "It's only a coconut." Her lack of surprise is the most worrying.

"How do you know that?"

She shrugs. "This is not my *first* time in the tropics. Come on, let's get out of here. We've lost the tail."

"What tail?" I plead.

She hot rods the golf cart through the gardens again. "This is cute. Maybe with a solar charge, it can . . . ."

"We're here," I interrupt her assessment of the golf cart, relieved to see Keston's sexy smile and Dex's warm one.

I put a hand on Mikah's arm.

"Is it true? Did I guess a secret you've been keeping from our friend group for twenty years? Are you an international spy?" I hear how ridiculous it sounds just saying it out loud.

In a somber vein, she says, "Do you know how many women are spies? A lot of housewives *and* . . . models. The people most of society overlook as clueless."

My mouth drops open. "That makes a perverse kind of sense."

"Besides," she says, catching my eye. "You're not the only one with a twenty-year-old secret."

I shut up. I hadn't told any of my friends I was pregnant and had a baby in college that I gave up for adoption until a few months ago. They've all said they understand. But I still feel guilty about it.

"You can't tell anyone," Mikah urges, and she's not the urgent type.

I do a cutting-my-throat-with-a-knife gesture. "Or else?"

"Exactly," says Mikah. "Now, let's go hang out with your lovely boyfriend. See what he's got on tap."

I sit for a moment, digesting the shocking news and adding it to all the other revelations I've had recently.

My friend is a spy. My boyfriend has a secret desire to kill a man who may be his brother. His ancestor is a pirate king with a hidden treasure. Or two. Not to mention, someone is following me and calling anonymously. Did I leave out anything?

As if reading my mind, Tabitha St. Clair goes strolling by, laptop under her arm and a cheery wave for my man at the bar.

Oh yeah, I forgot the ex.

Chapter Forty

ocoa Reef Resort's beach bar is becoming my second home. Even with Tabitha leaning across the polished wood, typing on her laptop, and photographing every damn cocktail Keston makes, I still feel as if I'm welcomed when I slide onto a stool and order one of Keston's fabulous rum punches.

Mellow reggae tunes have me bopping my head and tapping my fingers on the tabletop.

Keston throws a kiss across the teak counter. I wave and throw a kiss back.

Mikah takes it all in. She doesn't look like she's relaxing though. Her eyebrows are scrunched up under her sunglasses. Her foot taps a fast beat against the wooden drum that serves as a table for our drinks. Her breathing is shallow, like she's exerting herself.

"What's wrong?" I ask. "Do you think we're still being followed?"

"There's something fishy going on here," she says.

I point out Tabitha and explain she's Keston's ex-girlfriend. "Maybe her?" I say, slurping the drink through my straw. "*Probably* her."

Mikah shakes her head. She stirs her sparkling water with lime and leans on one beautiful hand to gaze around.

With the sunshine playing hide-and-seek, most tourists have bypassed the beach and settled in around the giant lima bean-shaped pool, which has dark blue umbrellas and matching loungers embroidered with the resort's name.

Dex and another server named Kay run between the beach bar and the pool, carrying trays full of sunset-colored cocktails. A few guests are dancing in the sand.

"No. I mean something *literally* fishy."

"Oh, the smell of fresh fish. Grilled tuna is on the menu today. It's yummy. They serve it with a pineapple salsa from the pineapples in the resort garden."

"Cool," she says, dropping her shoulders. "Everything on this island is fresh. Right out of the ground or sea."

Keston comes over with a big smile for us both. "Anything I can get you?"

I tap my glass. "This is amazing. You're upping your game, mister."

He kisses the tip of my sunburned nose. "All for you, my dear."

"There he is," Mikah says, her breath catching in her throat as she gazes over my shoulder. "I've been waiting for him to show himself."

She puts a hand on my arm. I'm not sure if it's to steady me or herself. I've never heard or seen Mikah breathless before.

Keston shifts his weight to encircle my shoulders and turns slowly. Almost as if he's expecting danger.

"What's going on over here?" asks a petulant voice. Tabitha slinks up to our table. Her eyes scan Mikah in a way I've seen other beautiful women size up Mikah as if hoping to find faults but failing.

I'm so concerned about how to introduce Mikah to Tabitha that I don't look to see who's got Mikah's undivided attention.

Until I hear a familiar low, slurry voice behind me.

"Hello, CJ. Can I talk to you?"

I gulp. Three other people at the table, and Kelley Harris Kips is only focused on me.

Mikah stretches out a hand. "Hi, I'm Mikah. You are?"

A long silence ensues.

I stand up from the table, fortified by Keston's strong rum punch. And by the desire to hear what Kelley Kips has to say.

"Hi." I don't deny knowing him this time. The cat is out of the bag.

I can feel Keston's energy thrumming through him like a tiger waiting to pounce. "It's okay," I whisper.

"Why were you following us?" asks Mikah warmly, as if she's happy to meet our stalker.

"You don't have to answer their questions," says Tabitha, standing protectively next to Kelley like a fine defense lawyer.

Except Kelley doesn't want or need defending. He steps back. I am mindful of what Alex said earlier. That Kelley may be on the spectrum. I'm unsure how that manifests itself, except he seems a bit lonely.

"Sure," I say. "Let's go over to one of the cabanas." I pick up my backpack with Charlotte's dairy in it. "Can my friend come too?" I indicate toward Mikah, who is practically salivating. Since when did Mikah drool over anyone?

He waves his hand in a movement I interpret as, "Sure."

"Don't worry, Keston," I whisper in what I hope is a reassuring manner. "It's only about the diary I found at your house. I've been trying to decipher stuff in there."

"I know what it's about," he says darkly. His eyes are as narrow as they can get without being closed.

I am aware that he possesses an alpha protective gene, but this isn't about being an alpha or even about me, really.

Keston harbors a deep wound where this man, who looks like him and shares his last name, is concerned. A wound that is peeling itself open slowly and surely. I can feel his pain. I just don't understand its source.

On an island where everyone knows everyone else's business, they also keep each other's secrets close to the vest.

Mikah leaps off her bar stool to follow me and Kelley.

"Should we go too?" I hear Tabitha asking Keston.

"No, I trust CJ to handle whatever it is."

Pride and affection swell within me. That's right, baby. We've got each other's backs.

"Plus, Mikah is going with her," he says practically.

I deflate like a beach ball that's been punctured.

Mikah links arms with me. "I'm in love," she whispers. "For the first time in my life."

I shake my head at her. "This is not the time for commentary, Mik. We've got some private business to attend to."

Her laugh is happy and suspicious at the same time, if that's possible.

"Private business or *pirate* business?" she asks. "Either way, love is always relevant. You said it yourself."

I don't answer because we've arrived at the cabana, and Kelley waits for us to enter.

I reach for the dairy and place it on the table. Kelley opens his beautifully woven messenger bag. It looks like something I can't afford. It is one of those all-natural accessories that celebrities carry to look down to earth. How the heck did Kelley Kips purchase it? Has he already found the buried treasure? Is he rich?

I gulp. *Don't jump ahead of yourself, CJ.*

He unwraps the book slowly, unwinding layers of the same beautiful rustic cloth to reveal an ancient dark leather book.

The one I have is scuffed and creased. This one looks as if it's been through a fire. Charred edges are visible, and it smells faintly of smoke and ash.

Who tried to burn the book?

"Is that the other diary?" I ask softly.

"For you," he says, pushing it toward me.

Part of me wants to grab it and turn the pages right away. Another part wonders about Kelley's reason for giving it to me.

"Why me?" I ask.

He puts a rough-hewn finger on top of the book. "It says so in there. When true love comes along, the diaries must be joined as one. It has been a long time. I was waiting for true love to show itself."

His one grey and one green eye look solemnly at me. Full of trust and something . . . virtuous or innocent. Almost otherworldly.

"True love?" I say, stalling. Is he talking about me and Keston? Or me and him? My heart thuds loudly. Better be me and Keston. I'm not about to divide two brothers, no matter how stunningly beautiful this one is.

In the silence, Mikah picks up a piece of the beige cloth the diary was wrapped in. "Excuse me. I am sorry to interrupt this book deal. But is this homemade all-natural woven hemp?" She handles the material as if it's the pirate gold itself.

Kelley's green and grey eyes turn bright and piercing like shards of glass. I wonder if he understands what she's asking him. I'm not sure I understand what she's asking.

"Did you *make* this cloth?" She presses.

He nods yes.

"How?"

"On my spinning wheel."

Mikah looks like she'll faint. "This is amazing. This is the softest, most tightly woven natural hemp I've seen. This would make great clothing."

He points to his pants that I previously thought were linen.

"You wove the hemp for this pair of pants?" Mikah asks. "Can I . . . touch them?"

Kelley stands up and pulls off his pants and hands them to Mikah. He is stark naked underneath.

"Guess they don't make hemp undies," I whisper from behind my hand.

Mikah is speechless.

Not that I'm staring or anything, but from the size of Kelley's well-endowed member, he is definitely related to Keston. In fact, if I peek a little further, I'd say they were twins.

Mikah's tongue is hanging out.

I reach over and close her mouth.

She silently hands Kelley back his pants. "They are very nice pants," she manages to say.

"Thank you. I learned how to make hemp clothing from

my grandfather. If you want, you can come to my farm. I'll show you how. It's on the other side of the island. My name is Kelley Kips. You will see a sign."

"Yes, please," Mikah nods her head hard.

To me, she whispers, "I may never come back."

Chapter Forty-One

I cradle both diaries in my hands as if they were newborns. I can't wait to read and compare them.

Is the second diary a continuation of Charlotte's? Or something different? Will the stories combine to shed light on Charlotte's romance? Or the location of Pirate Kipson's treasure? Or both?

All these questions merry-go-round their way in my head as I hurry back to the bar.

I leave Mikah and Kelley chatting under the shade of the thatched roof cabana. As far as I can tell, Kelley is not on the spectrum. He's a sexy hermit with a penchant for labor-intensive projects.

As I was packing up and leaving them, I overheard him telling Mikah about the bread he makes from cassava flour he harvests himself. The man is literally a Renaissance man living off the land. The exact opposite of Mikah's international supermodel/spy persona.

Kelley's introverted personality also seems to be the opposite of Keston's, who loves entertaining people and being part of the community. They're like yin and yang.

As soon as I return to the bar, Tabitha jumps off her stool and steps to me.

"Where's Kelley?" Her eyes dart around behind me.

I shrug. "Talking to my friend."

She looks rattled. "Kelley doesn't talk to people."

"He talked to me. He's talking to Mikah. He's changed his ways."

I don't mean to sound flippant. But there it is. My annoyance at Tabitha for the past three weeks has culminated in me brushing her off and striding past her.

She says fiercely, "You don't know anything about Kelley."

I swing around. Maybe it's frustration at Keston for not wanting to talk about Kelley. Or frustration that Tabitha is right, and I don't know anything, but I lose it.

"Just like I don't know anything about Keston, huh? Only you know everything. You're the best friend who picked up the pieces when I had to leave the island. I get it. You're Keston's protector. You're Kelley's protector. Which one of the brothers do you love, huh?"

"CJ!" Keston appears from behind the bar, his brown face drained of color. His eyes are wide. "What's going on?"

"That's what I'd like to know?" I whisper fiercely. "Why is *she* always here? Is there something going on between you guys? What will happen when I leave? Is she going to take my place?"

The moment my words tumble out, I regret them.

I can't believe I'm arguing with him at his job. Really? And laying my insecurities bare in front of Tabitha and Dex and anyone else close enough to hear.

This meltdown is because I'm afraid of what will happen when I get on a plane and say goodbye to Keston and St. Nicholas Island in less than two weeks.

The idea of leaving fills me with a dread I've been avoiding. But staying feels impossible. No job, no way to contribute. *Nada.*

And I feel left out of Keston's life. He has secrets about Kelley and about Tabitha. Why is our communication so awful?

"What happens *when* you leave is up to you," Keston says in a rough voice. "I did not ask you to move here . . . and I won't ask you to stay. Because I don't want you to look at me one day and resent giving up your old life for me. Either you're all in, or you aren't, and only you can decide that. You already know how I feel."

He turns and walks off, dropping his bar towel on the counter. "I'm going home now. You have your friend, your villa, and . . . my so-called brother." His last words come out bitter.

I stand in shock until I hear the loud rattling muffler of his motorbike zooming out of the employee parking lot behind the bar.

"Look what you did, Carmela Jones," Tabitha hisses.

"Me?" I try to keep my voice low. "What I did is fall in love with a man that you still love. But what I don't understand is why you are so . . . *concerned* about Kelley. If you love Keston."

Tabitha's hostile eyes bore right through me. "That isn't all you don't understand. Get your head out of your ass and do something to deserve Keston Kips."

I stagger backward. Her words hit home in a way I didn't know was possible. Am I undeserving of Keston?

The hatred in her eyes speaks volumes. Tabitha wants me off her island. I have officially made an enemy on St. Nicholas.

I recall Keston telling me when we were stranded together that life on a small island meant getting along. Everyone needs each other and helps each other out.

I'm alienating people left and right. Does that mean I don't belong here?

Tabitha flounces off and I feel like crying.

Dex's soothing sing-song voice says, "It'll be okay, CJ. Keston loves you. He only said all that because he's scared you'll leave him."

I turn to the quiet young man who is wise beyond his years. "Thank you, Dex. I'll fix this."

He nods. "You will. You have an invincible spirit."

"I don't know about that," I whisper. "I've messed up a lot." I wave goodbye to Dex and climb into the golf cart. My heart is heavy as I drive over to the cabana to collect Mikah and head back to the villa.

It's funny how I call it my villa but refer to Keston's home as "his." Have I been looking for excuses not to commit fully?

Which is dumb since I came all the way down here to be with him. But then started chickening out when life got real.

I have no one to blame but myself. I'm a forty-year-old woman in love with a thirty-two-year-old who I'm afraid is too young, has a different culture, and . . . let's see CJ, what other excuse do you have to disconnect from Keston?

Oh yeah, he has emotional issues he's not confronting.

Who the hell doesn't?

Chapter Forty-Two

Two days pass by with me hiding out in the villa, afraid of running into Keston, Tabitha, or anyone else who heard my outburst.

Keston is either mad at me for everything or giving me space. He hasn't called or texted, and I feel as if I should also give him space. I miss him terribly.

Mikah consoled me at first. When I told her I wanted to lay in the hammock and read the diaries, she seemed happy to take off to the other side of the island to learn about Kelley's off-the-grid lifestyle. I wonder if that's all she's learning about.

She's called daily to ask if I've stopped licking my wounds and am ready to emerge from my cave.

To which I remarked, "No."

Now she's leaving and I'm heading with her to the airport in a taxi. She's already said her goodbyes to Kelley. Turns out he bought his first cell phone ever to keep in touch with her.

"Which I think is him admitting he likes me," she says shyly.

"He didn't have a phone?" I ask amazed.

"Nope, you should see his place, CJ. It's an outdoor art gallery. So many sculptures. He works in textiles, clay, and anything he finds on the beach. I think he may be a genius."

I've never heard Mikah speak with wonder about anyone. I'm thrilled for her.

"Do you think you could ever live on St. Nicholas?" I venture as the taxi slows to enter the airport.

She looks at the bright blue sea on the left side and the green hills on the right. The airstrip sits in between them.

"I don't know. What would I do here?"

"That's what I keep asking myself," I exclaim, glad to have someone who understands.

"But then again, CJ," she says, climbing out of the taxi and stretching her long limbs to the sky. "Why do we have to have all the answers before we take a leap? Isn't that the opposite of trusting yourself?"

Her words linger in my head as I squeeze her in the tightest hug. "Thank you for coming," I whisper. "And be careful doing you know what."

"You be careful you don't lose that gorgeous man."

"Point taken," I mutter. "What's going to happen between you and Kelley?"

Her eyes turn dreamy. "I'm going to convince him to come to Paris. I have friends who would love to meet him. See his portfolio."

"He has a portfolio?" I ask, wondering how a man without a phone could have that.

"He will," says Mikah.

"Don't ruin him," I say sincerely. "He's an innocent."

"He's the real treasure of St. Nicholas," she says with a wide smile. "No one can ruin him."

I think about her words all the way back to the resort. The *real* treasure of St. Nicholas.

Are Kelley and Keston, the descendants of a true love? Because I've worked it out myself. From bits and pieces of what I know. Keston's father must have had an affair with Mrs. Harris. Maybe they bonded over their shared interest in finding the pirate treasure.

She must have given birth to Kelley a few months before Keston was born. Mikah said Kelley's birthday is in March. I know Keston's birthday is in May of the same year, making them half-brothers.

Being only two months apart, Kelley sometimes calls them "twins." It's the only thing that makes sense. It explains why they look so much alike.

Maybe Keston denies that Kelley is his brother because his father cheated on his mother.

It would explain why Kelley would have the flask and the other diary.

But what is the treasure? And more importantly, where is it?

I stay up most of the night, pouring over the diaries, the one belonging to Charlotte Campbell, and the other, which has turned out to be a ship captain's log from 1803 to 1804. Kipson's ship log to be exact.

When I try to sleep, I dream the same dream over and over.

It starts off the same as the last one I had. I'm following a man who turns around. He looks like Kelley and Keston. But older. Rougher. With prominent cheekbones. Wild eyes in a dark face.

Waves hit the rock he's standing on. This time a woman in a long cloak appears next to him.

Something is terribly wrong. She's crying. Seems to be in great pain. He's holding her hand. Helping her toward a cave. Before they enter, he turns around and opens his hand.

Gold coins glitter in the dark. He drops them at the entrance of the cave.

A huge wave smacks the rocks as they disappear inside. A bright blue glow illuminates the water around the cave. Blue stars shine in the sea, showing them the way.

Then everything goes dark.

I sit up with a gasp. "Oh my God. I know that light."

Turning on the bedside lamp, I sit cross-legged and turn to the pages that have been haunting me all day and night.

Chapter Forty-Three

June 12th, 1803

Anchored in the shadows of St. Nicholas tonight, a hidden gem away from prying eyes and the King's men. This island, cloaked in its wild greenery, serves more than just a refuge. It harbors my greatest treasure—not of gold or silver, but of heart and spirit.

Under cover of darkness, I stole away to the secret cove where the sea sparkles with living light, as if the stars themselves decided to swim in the waters. There, waiting, was my beloved Charlotte. She claims to be a maid in the home of a Scottish lord. But I know her real birthright. A princess of the King's country and daughter of my sworn enemy. Would she but mine to take and keep?

She knows who I am—what I am. Yet her eyes hold no fear, only the burning truth that she, too, is a creature not meant for a tame and tethered life. In her company, I am not the feared pirate captain, but simply a man with a heart capable of more than plunder.

Tonight, as my ship makes haste, the path illuminated by the shimmering sea, I carry with me the warmth of our shared moments, a silent vow to return as the wheel of time permits.

These lines come only after pages and pages of boring details about the ship, its men, and life dipping in and out of coves and bays. There are only a few passages about his love for Charlotte. But his love is deep and if they could be together, they would.

In August 1803, he returned to St. Nicholas and wrote:

Our love is not one for the faint of heart; it is as tempestuous as any Caribbean storm. We speak little of the morrow, for in our private world, the morrow is as uncertain as the winds of time. Instead, we speak of dreams bigger than both of us—freedom, a life together, even children to hold dear.

As I write this in the dim light of my cabin, the ship hidden away behind the dark folds of the hills, I am reminded why I return to St. Nicholas, why I risk my freedom. For those stolen hours in Charlotte's embrace, I am more than my reputation, more than my deeds. And as I set sail at dawn, the echo of her sweet voice and the promise of return will be the wind in my sails.

My heart hurts for them. Theirs was a forbidden love and a doomed relationship.

But at least now I know that Kipson and Charlotte's secret meeting place was where Keston took me to see the bioluminescence. That has to be the meaning of the words, "*where the sea sparkles with living light, as if the stars themselves decided to swim in the waters.*" Blue light. It's what I saw in my dream.

My subconscious was busy deciphering the diaries where my conscious brain could not.

My entire body tingles as I turn the pages, reading slowly and carefully so I don't miss a word. Even after I finish reading, I start over and read each page again. I must be missing something. Their love has no end. Where is the mention of a treasure?

Why does Charlotte's diary stop abruptly? Her last entry reads:

Love grows in beauteous ways. And dies the same way.

Like, what the hell, Charlotte? You can't leave me hanging like that. I close my eyes and focus on the image of the woman in my dream. She was covered in a long cloak. She had red hair. Her eyes were far away. But looked green. Or grey. Or green and grey. Like Kelley's. I can't trust my subconscious.

I open her diary again and read each page the way I'd read each piece of evidence in one of my cases.

The words circling in my head are: *What am I not seeing?*

Chapter Forty-Four

Often, we cannot see clearly what is right in front of our eyes. I learned as a lawyer to look for patterns in how a person communicates for clues to hidden meanings.

It could be a person's tone, their word choices, or what they avoid saying. Reading over Charlotte Campbell's diary a third and fourth time, I see a pattern I had noticed but ignored.

Charlotte was sick a lot. She mentioned having "the curse" often in March and April.

She mentions it repeatedly. I'd assumed she was pretending to be sick to get away from her family and sneak off to meet Kipson. But she had "the curse" a lot again between September and December. I thought the curse was her period, but now I think it was the exact opposite.

Charlotte Campbell was *pregnant* for most of 1803. How could I have missed that? She talked about the intimacies she shared with Captain Kipson starting in January 1803. Her curse could easily be morning sickness or pregnancy issues.

Oh dear, poor Charlotte. I clutch my throat. I, too, kept a pregnancy hidden. I had my baby and didn't tell anyone. Did Charlotte do the same thing? Did she feel as ashamed as I had?

If Charlotte was pregnant and unmarried, she probably kept it a secret until the end. But what happened when it was time to deliver? Did she have her baby alone?

And what happened to the baby? Was he the pirate's son who grew up on his father's ship like Keston mentioned? The one who returned to St. Nicholas to purchase the treasure hidden in plain sight—the Kipson land?

My heart races with the pieces of the puzzle falling into place.

I get up, stretch, eat room service, and pace the villa's thick carpeted floors. My brain is working on borrowed time here. As if my own relationship hinges on unraveling the mystery of Kipson and Charlotte's love affair.

Assuming Charlotte was pregnant, I reread Captain Kipson's ship log for clues about what happened to her or the baby. He had to have known.

But I come up with nothing. It was such a lovely narrative by a man who was a ruthless pirate of the Caribbean seas. He was tough with everyone except his beloved.

He'd have made plans for her, somehow. He would not have deserted his Charlotte. Same with Keston. He'd never turn his back on me.

When I'm tired of being indoors, I head outside and pace on the warm sand bordering the villa's patio. I tread channels, going back and forth, thinking about what my next move should be.

Her pregnancy probably explains why he came to St. Nicholas so often in 1803 and why this is the only log preserved as part of the Kipson heritage.

"He loved her so much," I whisper to the hummingbirds as they whirl from flower to flower, their iridescent wings blazing like jewels in the sun. While the birds zip around and show off, small lizards blend into the rocks hiding in plain sight.

Hiding in plain sight!

I flip the pages of the ship log until I get to December 24, 1803. This is the most difficult section to read. In fact, impossible. The words are jumbled. But what if he hid a message in plain sight?

Every time I take a break from reading the diaries, I hide them. Sometimes under my mattress, sometimes wrapped in clothing and tucked away in a drawer. Most times, I stack them under a lamp as if they're innocent books, hiding in full view of anyone who enters.

Captain Kipson was a shrewd pirate and captain of his own ship, *The Scarlet Tempest.* He'd known about hiding in plain view.

I stare at the pages intently until I sink into the words themselves. My pesky inner voice says, "What if you turn them upside down?"

Turning the old heavy journal, I squint at scribbles in between the lines until I realize they form words and sentences. But none of it is legible. Until I turn the page of the upside-down book to see what's on the back of the entry.

Suddenly, what was a mess of scribbles transforms into words. Captain Kipson wrote a whole other entry, dated December 24, 1803, in an upside-down, right-to-left script for no one to see but himself.

In fact, anyone reading the log would skip over the entry because it looks like gibberish. Like the ship was rocking hard and his hand was unsteady. But I've gotten used to reading his handwriting.

I read the secret entry quickly, my heart hammering in my chest. Tears brim and fall at his brave words. Two hundred and twenty years later, I'm standing outside, the sun beating on my head, but I feel every emotion Captain Kipson felt.

About his beloved Scarlett Tempest, not only his ship's name but also the name he called Charlotte Campbell during childbirth.

He was there. Like I knew he would be. He'd risk anything for her—even his freedom.

A sudden loud ringing interrupts my musings.

"Yes?" I answer my cell phone a bit crossly.

"Hello, this is Kelley Harris Kips."

"Kelley, I know who you are. Thank goodness you called. I have a question for you."

"I'm ready."

I imagine Kelley in his homemade hemp clothing, unbothered by anything, standing with a cell phone in his hand and wondering how to use it.

"Did you know Charlotte Campbell was pregnant with Captain Kipson's baby in 1803?"

Dead silence on the other end.

"Are you there?"

A throat clears. "Yes. I am here. I'm . . . shocked."

I'm shocked he's shocked.

Isn't the myth that Keston (and Kelley too) are the sons of a pirate king and a Scottish princess? So, at some point, Charlotte had to get pregnant?

Yet, it seems neither Kelley nor I expected it.

"I just found a hidden entry in the ship log you gave me. In Captain Kipsons's handwriting." I take my time saying the next sentence.

"It's about the birth of Charlotte and Kipson's offspring."

Silence.

"Kelley?"

"No one's ever found anything like that," he whispers.

I clear my throat. "There's more, but I don't want to discuss it over the phone."

"I'll be there as soon as I can. Give me about two hours."

"Okay."

This is what I need. To share my discovery with someone to whom this story matters more than just a hunt for treasure.

"What you *need* to do is talk to Keston," my subconscious shouts at me.

"Fine! I will!"

My watch says it's three o'clock, so he should be at the beach bar.

I change into one of the sexy sundresses Mikah left with me. It has a bustier top, revealing mounds of flesh, and a skater skirt, showing off my darkly tanned legs. I slip on the strappy gold sandals she left me, which are a tad too loose, and I'm ready.

My jeans, tank, and beloved pink Vans will have to take a backseat for now.

I look around vainly, trying to find a peace offering to give Keston. A white flag gift. I only have the diaries. I pack them into my backpack and head out on foot to get there quicker by cutting across the lawn instead of driving along the pathways.

Chapter Forty-Five

The air is warm and shimmering with heat mirages. The storm we expected a few days ago never materialized. Hopefully, it's not still making its way toward St. Nicholas.

As I step closer to the bar, goosebumps trail down my arms.

When I'm right behind it, Keston's deep rumbling bass causes my eyes to water. I missed him so much.

His hugs, his kisses, and chatting as friends. Not to mention his hot lovemaking. He's spoiled me forever.

I let myself drift into the sing-song voice I know so well. Was this how Charlotte felt when she was waiting for Captain Kipson? Her heart pumping furiously. Hands clammy. Stomach feeling like a balloon floating up to the sky.

"CJ?"

My eyelids snap open.

A radiant smile spreads across Keston's face as if he's unable to contain his joy. "You came!"

Before I can say a word, he grabs me in his arms and lifts me off my feet in a giant hug. When I'm back on my two feet, I try to tell him how sorry I am. "I want to say . . . ." My voice cracks. My fingers twist nervously at my side.

"Shut up, woman, you're here. It'd better be because you couldn't stand another moment without me."

"I couldn't," I cry. "It was awful. But you need to give me a chance to say what I came to say."

He crosses his arms and leans against the wall of the bar. "Hit it."

I screw up my nose. "I forgot how irritating you can be."

He drops his cool stance and snatches me off my feet again. Nuzzles his face into my neck. "Is this irritating?" he asks, kissing me wildly, per usual not caring who sees us.

"Oh, my goodness, Kes, can you let me breathe?"

"No," he says firmly. "I let you breathe for three days. While I was underwater drowning."

"It was two."

"Felt like ten."

Dex nods vigorously coming up behind Keston. "You better

not make the staff suffer like that again, CJ. He was unbearable."

I smack Keston's arm. "Meanie."

"Your fault."

"Take responsibility for your own actions."

That's too much for him. He unhooks the backpack from my shoulders and tosses it over his own.

With one move, he slides his arm under my legs and hoists me into the air. "You're coming with me. You've been a very bad girl. Dex, close out my shift."

He doesn't wait for an answer and instead starts walking toward the beach.

My eyes open wide. "What're you going to do?"

He looks at the sky. "First a little spanking. Then a lot of loving. Or we can switch the order, but there's definitely a spanking."

"I don't condone violence," I say haughtily.

He kisses my lips as he walks down the beach, heading to where the river meets the sea.

"Then you shouldn't misbehave."

"But I have something important to tell you," I say.

"And I have something important to do to you." His eyebrows waggle up and down.

I sigh. "It's no use arguing with you when you're horny."

"That's more like it. Now, be a good girl and kiss me back."

I close my eyes and open my mouth under his probing tongue. He sucks my lips until they're bruised. His teeth nip at the corners of my mouth. His tongue tangles with mine as if he's feasting on me.

His kisses consume my very core. My entire body relaxes under his mouth and hands. I feel as if I'm floating, yet every nerve ending is shouting for a release.

"Baby," he whispers when we reach the bleached rocks

lining the riverbed. A gentle flow of water steams through the rocky path.

Keston splashes through the river and sets me down on a flat rock.

Mischief twinkles in his eyes. He fingers the sundress. Nods appreciatively. "Thanks for making this easy."

I roll my eyes. "I wasn't trying to make anything easy for you."

A finger wags in my face. "Don't make me spank you harder than you already deserve, young lady."

A giggle escapes my mouth. "I've never been spanked."

Keston searches the riverbanks.

"What are you doing?"

"What do you think?"

I shrug.

"Ha! Found it."

Did he seriously find a stick to spank me with?

I cover my knees with my arms feeling exposed in this flimsy dress while sitting on a rock in the middle of the rain forest.

"Can we negotiate?" I plead.

"You look like a defiant fairy," a slow grin lights up his handsome face. "Like you're packing fairy weapons under that magic skirt."

"Maybe I am. Are you open to a negotiation?"

He shakes his head. "The answer is a hard no." He strokes the front of his pants. "Emphasis on hard."

"Ha!" I laugh. "You got jokes."

He stops stripping the leaves off the branch he'd picked up.

"Besides, you have nothing to negotiate with. You have no leverage. Do you realize you left me for *four* days?"

"It was *two!*"

"Turn over and show me that sweet ass."

"You're serious?"

He smacks his palm with the branch. It sounds serious.

He twirls his hand in the classic, "turn around" signal.

I bite my lip. Reach out a tentative hand and stroke the front of his pants where his massive member strains to push itself out.

He shudders. "Evil woman."

"Good man."

I slowly slide down the zipper of his pants. His arms drop to his sides. The spanking branch tumbles from his hand.

"Oh, CJ," he moans as I stroke the dark one-eyed monster protruding from his underwear.

The tip is swollen and a drop of precum shimmers on the wide opening. I lick it up before sliding his underwear down and taking his cock in my mouth. My fingers find the base. I grip it as if grabbing a pot off the stove.

My tongue and mouth take sweet turns. I circle the tip with my tongue. Then slide my mouth as far down his cock as I can go without gagging.

It's all lick, suck, slide, over and over, my rhythm making him moan and pump his hips sliding his dick further and further into my mouth.

I open wide and breathe deeply to take it.

His hands clutch at my hair.

This is the largest cock I've ever sucked. It keeps growing in my mouth like a heat-seeking missile.

"Good Lord, Keston," I whisper as I come up for air. "Your cock is so sweet and juicy with milk."

"Better than a spanking?" he whispers.

"Much better," I murmur my lips sliding around the pulsating member.

As I suck and lick, he fingers my hard nipples. Hot sensations zip to my pussy. It's crying to get in on the action.

My breasts escape the sundress. He weighs them, plucks the

nipples, squeezes them tightly then runs one hand down my belly to find my pussy.

Hallelujah!

His rough fingers play with my clit. He inserts a finger into my dripping flower. I whimper and suck his cock.

We're getting into a frenzy. Moaning sounds come from both of us. With my eyes closed I slurp up the slickness on the tip of his cock. I take the massive dick deep into my throat and let him fuck my mouth.

"Oh lord, CJ!" he shouts right before a stream of hot cum explodes and runs down my throat. I swallow some but it's too much and too hot. I can't take it all. But I want to try. For him.

He opens his eyes and watches me slide my tongue around the rim licking up the last bits.

"You're amazing sweetheart," he whispers. "Now turn around."

"Still? I thought I served my punishment."

"We're not done."

He flips up the back of my dress and pushes his penis into my plumped and waiting hole. He's still hard. I'm shocked.

He puts one foot up on the rock for leverage. He grips my hips from behind and slides his sweet dick all the way out until only the tip is teasing my pussy.

"I want it all," I moan.

"You've been a very bad girl. You only get the tip."

"Not fair."

His rough hand presses on my clit and then releases the pressure. It's his signature move, and it drives me crazy. Press, release. Press, release. Meanwhile, his cock slides in a tiny bit then slides back out. It's pure agony.

"Give me the goddamn dick already," I huff.

A laugh ripples through him. "I should make you beg but . . . ."

He slides his cock all the way in and sighs. "It's too damn good."

It only takes a few pumps of his lovely cock to make me scream and writhe with ecstasy. My pussy throbs around his cock, making him pump harder until he, too, is shouting for mercy in the darkening forest.

I drop onto the rock face and weep with relief. My body is spent. My mind is clear. My heart is free.

I gaze at him across the rock where he's laid out flat. He ruffles my curls with one hand.

"You can be bad anytime you want, darling."

I smile at my man. His cock rests like a smooth dark seal across his lower abs. I stroke it gently. "You really got a prize here, dude."

"That makes you the winner then."

"It does indeed," I agree. "It does indeed."

Chapter Forty-Six

"Are we going to talk about what happened at the bar with Tabitha that caused our . . . disagreement?" he asks as we wash off in the river and get dressed.

Well, no clothes were removed, so it's more of a pulling up and pulling down. My beautiful dress has a rip, though.

"When are we going to make love inside a room again? On a real bed?"

He blinks. "People do that?"

I laugh and smack his arm. "I'd like to try it out more often."

"I'll put it on the agenda. Are you avoiding the topic?"

"Me? You're the one who didn't want to talk about Kelley. Now you want me to talk about Tabitha?"

"We're not having any more misunderstandings," Keston says firmly. "Enough is enough, don't you agree."

"I do, baby. I hated fighting with you. Let's promise no more secrets, no more hiding things."

"I promise," he says and kisses my lips. "This is what communication looks like. If you argue with me again, I am definitely spanking you."

I giggle. "And vice versa."

He pretends to consider the idea with a gleam in his eye.

In one sense it is good we're having a few disagreements so we can learn how to resolve them. On the other hand, we're wasting precious time together.

He shakes out his t-shirt, twigs flying everywhere. Sunlight streams through the trees making leaf shadows dance on his abs.

"Gorgeous much?" I grumble.

"What are you muttering, my little fairy queen?"

I pat down my hair and slide on some lip gloss. "Nothing."

We stroll hand in hand down the beach. Our feet crunch sand as the wind off the waves ruffles our hair.

"Does it look like another storm is coming?" I ask fearfully, checking the sky.

His hand tightens on mine. "One might. It's okay, baby. We can stay in. We don't have to go anywhere. We will make popcorn, watch golf on TV, and make love *indoors*."

"Golf! I'd rather brave the weather."

He smacks a big kiss on my shoulder. "Golf is sexy. Give it a chance. It's all in the way you swivel your hips." He grabs my hips and turns them in a sexy side-to-side motion. "Hot, no?"

"You're the only person I've met who equates golf with sex. The ONLY one."

"Wait until you see me play!"

"You'd probably look sexy throwing *darts*."

He flexes his biceps in front of my eyes. Imitating a dart-throwing arm. Then grins in my face. "You like?"

I smack his muscles down. "Show off."

As we approach the resort, he slings an arm over my shoulder. "So, what's on the agenda? Because as that song goes . . . ." He starts singing aloud the classic by the reggae group Third World. "*Now that we've found love, what are we gonna do with it.*"

I join in because it's infectious and the lyrics are on point.

Our voices rise out of key happily.

Until we reach the beach bar.

"What is he doing here?" Keston growls.

"What is she doing here?" I snarl at the same time.

Kelley is drinking coconut water. His unruly hair is neatly held back with a colorful hair band. I swallow my comment about his strong resemblance to Keston when Keston wears his bandanas.

Next to Kelley, Tabitha pretends like she's about to step into a *Love is Blind* pod, where true love awaits. I resist the urge to roll my eyes at her.

"I have something to tell you," I say nervously to Keston.

"Whatever it is, I'm not leaving your side. Four days was an eternity."

"It was two!" I swear under my breath. "Anyway, you may not like what I'm doing. Or going to do." My tongue is having a hard time forming the words I need.

"As long as it doesn't involve *him,* I'm all in." He indicates with his chin who "him" is.

I drag Keston off to the side of the bar, where no one can see us.

Or, hopefully, hear us.

"Kelley and I are going to look for the pirate treasure," I blurt.

His face storms up. "Over my dead body. My father died looking for that treasure with *him.*"

"Who?"

"That man."

"I didn't know that last part," I say softly, touching his shoulder to steady his shaking body.

"Now you do. I forbid it."

I step back. "Let's not fight again, please. You can't forbid me from doing anything."

"Fine," he says heatedly. "I strongly urge . . . no, I *beg* you not to do it."

"I think I owe it to Charlotte Campbell and Captain Kipson to find it. They are your ancestors. They were madly in love, Keston. I'm learning a lot from reading their journals."

I clutch the backpack closer to my body.

"It's the most beautiful love story, but sad and painful, and if I can find the treasure, maybe it could help us. Maybe their doomed love was for a reason. To bring wealth to our lives. So we can live together on this island without worry. And help Kel . . . and *others.*"

I hear myself rambling out reasons why it's okay for me to

go in search of his family treasure—against his wishes—but I strongly feel like this is my destiny.

Keston locks eyes with mine. "*You* are my wealth. *You* are my treasure. I cannot lose you, CJ." His voice breaks.

"Then come with us," I say boldly. "We could use your help."

"We're all coming," says the voice I detest most in the world. Her uppity sing-song tone grates like a fingernail on a chalkboard.

"Grab your stuff, let's go," Tabitha orders. "Keston, you need to do this for your family. Kelley needs to finish what he started. And you . . . Carmela Jones."

I stare at the wicked witch of St. Nicholas. "Yes?"

"We can't do it without you. Kelley says you discovered a secret that has stumped the Kips and Campbell families for centuries."

"We're not talking about a treasure hunt here," I say. "Let's go to my villa. I mean *the* resort's villa."

Fortunately, no one objects, and Tabitha, Keston, and Kelley follow me to the fancy whitewashed building. I let us in through the patio doors. Housekeeping came while I was gone.

My room service trays have disappeared, and my bed is made up.

"Take a seat," I say before collapsing on a love seat, mentally and physically exhausted.

The energy in the room is not a "we're part of a small island and must work together" vibe like Keston says is the norm on St. Nicholas.

Far from it.

Keston stands next to my chair. Kelley leans against the patio door, staring out at the sea. Tabitha makes tea as if this is her room.

I don't argue. I'm coming to realize she's not going anywhere. She's a nasty cold I can't get rid of.

Meanwhile, Keston is staring daggers at Kelley, which is ineffective because Kelley is oblivious or used to being hated.

Seeing Kelley empty-handed, I remembered his flask and searched my suitcase for it.

"Thanks, CJ," he says, opening it and taking a swig.

Keston's face turns purple.

"That's my father's flask."

"Mine, too," says Kelley, cool as beans.

Tabitha claps her hands.

"Cool it."

I raise my hand. "I get why Keston and Kelley may want to search for their ancestor's treasure, but why should *you* come along?"

"Because," Tabitha hesitates as if weighing what to say. Her light brown skin is infused with red. I've never seen her blush.

Kelley nods encouragingly. "You should tell her."

"Charlotte Campbell was my five-times great-grandmother."

"Whoa! I didn't see that coming."

"I told you everyone here is connected in some crazy fashion," Keston says. "Although we're not all blood relatives." He gives a nod to Tabitha. Then he glares at Kelley. "While some are but shouldn't be."

"Charlotte married a Scottish nobleman when she was in her mid-twenties," Tabitha intervenes quickly. "He was a governor of St. Nicholas. I'm from that line of descendants. Although the myth about her being involved with a pirate before her marriage has marred her reputation for centuries."

"It is no myth. She was involved. She had his child."

Keston and Tabitha gasp in unison.

"I also have information that can lead us to the pirate's treasure. But we should go soon . . . maybe tonight."

Keston's voice is pained when he says, "Sorry, CJ, I can't participate in anything that involves him."

Tabitha makes a tut-*tut* noise in her throat and focuses her beautiful green eyes on Keston.

"You already are participating in something that involves him."

"What?"

"*Everything!* Breathing. Being here with your girlfriend."

Wow! She acknowledges I'm Keston's girlfriend. Finally.

"What are you talking about, Tabby?" Keston scowls at her. "I don't have anything to do with this guy who showed up at my father's funeral with a crazy story of how they were treasure hunting and how he's Kellum Kips's *other* son—causing a scene at his funeral! My poor mother and sister. They couldn't take the pity and the questions from all the islanders. You know it's why they moved away."

Kelley takes another long sip of dandelion wine as if the discussion has nothing to do with him. I need to master his zen and the art of not being bothered.

"He was fourteen. Same as you. He was sad. Same as you."

Tabitha drops onto a stool and glances around to see if everyone is paying attention.

"He was Dad's goddamn secret child," Keston shouts.

From Tabitha's shocked expression, I don't think she's ever heard Keston Kips raise his voice. He sounds as if his heart is being ripped out of his chest.

Tears shine in his eyes. His hands curl into fists at his sides. "I hated him for that. I hated you for telling us," he spits that last part in Kelley's direction.

No one says a word.

Kelley walks over to Keston and tries to hand him the flask. "I didn't know about you either until his funeral. My mother tried to stop me from going. I didn't understand why. I thought I was his only son."

Kelley's eyes are haunted and bleak. Reflecting the look in his brother's own.

Tabitha's own eyes fill with tears. "I didn't know that. You never told me that."

"I never told anyone. The entire island stopped talking to me after the funeral. Even my mother. That's why I moved out to my grandfather's land. He died when I was eighteen. I never left until . . . , " he stops and looks at Tabitha, "you came and got me."

Both young men had lost more than their father. They'd lost their entire lives as they knew it.

"Secrets are horrible," I cry.

Three pairs of eyes stare dismally at me.

I was never the cheerleader type. In fact, I'm the opposite. My favorite dwarf is Grumpy. My favorite Sesame Street character is Oscar.

I dig deep. "Guys, you were both harmed by your father's secrets. Not to speak ill of the dead, but he was wrong to hide your existence from each other, which could not have been easy on this small island. I can't imagine how horrible it must have been for you both to discover the truth at his funeral.

"What's not horrible, however, is when two people love each other more than life itself. They devote themselves to each other and dream of something bigger and better than their love. Something their love can inspire. Even if it doesn't happen in their lifetime.

"I'm talking about the love between Captain Kipson and Charlotte Campbell. It's why we are standing here, talking to each other. The mystery of their love has brought you two here.

"They would want their descendants to be happy. They gave up a lot when they could not be together."

Strangely, Tabitha claps her hands. "That's the kind of love I want."

"Me too," says Keston, reaching for my hand.

"Me, three," says Kelley, gazing out the patio window.

"Then let's go find it. Because there's proof that kind of love existed, and I know the way."

Chapter Forty-Eight

"Can you hurry up?" I ask Tabitha, who is taking off her shoes, rolling up her pant legs, tucking her hair into a ponytail, and basically doing everything possible to delay our departure.

The sun has set its fiery orb into the sea leaving behind a sky glowing with grape and tangerine brush strokes. The air is hot as if the day hasn't cooled itself off yet.

Keston's boat engine roars loudly, sending Trixie skittering from the wooden jetty back onto the porch where she was snoring her little heart out when we arrived half an hour ago.

Trixie brayed loudly when she first saw me. I brayed back. We had a hug and I gave her carrots to apologize for my absence.

"I'm not leaving you again," I whispered in her ear.

Keston overheard and grinned. "She better not, right Trixie Starlight?"

I rolled my eyes at him.

Now, with Tabitha finally in the boat, Kelley unties the line for us and hops in next to me and Keston. Tabitha is seated on the bench near the bow.

"What's our destination, captain?" Keston asks me.

"The lagoon. Where the bioluminescence lights up the water."

"Is this a sightseeing cruise?" Tabitha scoffs.

I shake my head. Over the steady hum of the boat engine, I begin to tell them the tale of a long-ago love involving Kelley and Keston's legendary forebear, Captain Kipson. And Tabitha's irrepressible matriarch, Charlotte Campbell.

"Imagine being a pirate sailing this same sea on the way to meet your true love."

I look at Tabitha. "A love who waited on the shore where the river meets the sea, and the water lights up with a bright blue light."

"The lagoon was their meeting point?" Keston asks, surprise making his eyes round. "I go there all the time."

I nod. "Where the freshwater meets the salty sea."

"It's amazing she could find her way out there by land," says Tabitha. "It's a difficult trek even in the daytime."

"The things we do for love," Kelley says.

We all turn to stare at him.

He smiles. "I know a little about love. It changes you."

I wonder if he's thinking of Mikah. I can't see this cool, relaxed man in the hustle and bustle of a big city. But Mikah may convince him after all.

"Anyway," I say, smiling at Kelley, "Charlotte and Captain Kipson met at their secret spot on the shore. They talked and shared their dreams. He adored her. He let his guard down and spoke freely about his rough and dangerous life. She told him about her strict and rigid one.

"Together they escaped their regular lives and were free. They became intimate, sharing a deep passion for each other. Charlotte was fierce about her love for him. She declared to her diary that he was her true love, despite being a feared outlaw."

Tabitha shakes her head. "Poor Grams. In love with a bad boy."

"The worst," Keston says. "Bottom of the barrel in suitable husbands."

"During one of those intimate encounters, Charlotte Campbell became pregnant with Captain Kipson's child."

Tabitha all but chokes on the water she was sipping. "No." She wipes the drops away. "My fine upstanding Grams, a Governor's wife, got knocked up before she met my Grands?"

"By a pirate," says Keston.

"A Black pirate," Kelley adds.

"Yes, Charlotte Campbell of the illustrious Campbell plantation, a princess with a silver spoon in her mouth, was with child."

"The scandal," Tabitha murmurs.

"They kept it a secret. As far as I can tell, no one knew."

Keston locks eyes with me. "You, okay?" He mouths silently.

I nod. My heart is full of love for this man. Every day will not be perfect or even close to perfect, but we will always have our shared love.

"Then, in December of the same year, it was time for Charlotte to give birth. I don't know how they arranged to meet at the right time. It appears Captain Kipson stayed in and around St. Nicholas's waters, risking his life to be near his beloved when she needed him most."

Tabitha swoons, grasping her heart with both hands. "That is true love."

I take a breath and a sip from my water bottle.

"You're good at telling the story, CJ," Keston remarks, eyes focused ahead, but a smile just for me. "Remember when you read your romance novels to me?"

"We were stranded. You were a captive audience."

He laughs. "I loved it."

It's Tabitha's turn to roll her eyes. "Please continue."

"I found evidence about the birth in Captain Kipson's ship log. It was written in a secret way, hidden in plain sight but invisible to most."

"Except to you," Kelley says. "I found a note in his journal that said:

If your heart has found a love that's true,
If your souls are joined as one,
Then you may find the hidden treasure,
Of a love that can't be measured.

"Wow! I exclaim. "It said that?"

Kelley nods. "I memorized it. That's why I gave you the journal. I saw you at the hospital the day you both were rescued from No Man's Land. I heard you crying over Keston. Your words and emotions made everyone cry."

"I don't remember much of that day," I murmur. "It was one of the worst days of my life."

"I knew you and Keston had the kind of true love the journal talked about. I hoped you would figure out the secret. And you did," Kelley says.

Keston turns around, one hand still on the steering wheel. "Why were you at the hospital?"

Kelley grows silent.

"They sent me to find him," Tabitha speaks up.

Keston stares at one, then the other. He slows down the engine. Turns it off.

"Are we here?" I ask.

"Yes, baby. It's right over there."

I look to the empty darkness looming ahead of us. "Scary."

Keston looks at Tabitha and Kelley. "Why'd you have to find him?"

I don't understand the tension in the air. What's the big deal with Kelley being at the hospital anyway?

A couple of beats go by.

Kelley looks up at the sky. "The doctors asked me to donate blood for your surgeries."

Tabitha and I swivel our heads from one brother to the other as if watching a tennis match.

"Did you?" Keston asks in a hushed voice.

"Yes. I did. We have the same blood type. O-negative. We can only receive blood from each other or another O-negative donor. They were short on O-negative blood."

"Was it just once?"

Kelley purses his lips. "Three times. One for every surgery you had."

"I didn't know."

Kelley shrugs.

"I lost a lot of blood on No Man's Land. I almost died. You saved my life, thank you."

Kelley waves his thanks away.

I gulp. Keston *literally* has Kelley's blood in him. It looks as if he realizes that because he walks over to Kelley and sticks out his hand to shake. "No, seriously, thank you."

Kelley grips Keston's hand. "You're welcome."

Tabitha and I exchange looks that don't kill. We're all making progress here under a starless sky.

Keston hugs me and kisses the top of my head. "I suppose since we're all revealing truths, secrets, whatever you want to call them . . . I have one for CJ."

I perk up as if I'm getting a present.

"It's about what Tabitha and I have been doing together."

My perkiness dies a swift death. "Do I want to know?"

The rocking boat gets smacked by a wave on her starboard side, almost tumbling me off my seat. Keston tucks an arm around me. "I got you."

He then proceeds to tell me all about his and Tabitha's special project. A book of rum cocktails he has been working on for years. But now he's inspired to finish it because of me.

"Filled with new drinks, sexy names, lots of photos and information about the ingredients."

"That sounds amazing," I hug him hard. "I'm so proud of you."

"It's just about ready. Can you help me prepare it for the printers?"

"Yes!" I say happily.

"We will sell it everywhere. At the resorts and bars in town, even online. What do you think?"

"It's wonderful. People would love to have a book of your creations. What are you doing with the money?" I ask quietly.

Keston bends over to peer into my eyes. "It's for you, my love. To expand our house. Get a vehicle. Buy more carrots for Trixie. I want you to relax and stop worrying about our *finances.*" He snickers. "Take the time to figure out what you love to do."

"I already found my treasure," I say, burying my face in his shirt so everyone doesn't see my tears. I love this man so much.

"I know I found mine," he whispers. "Although you're a pain in my neck."

"Nobody's perfect," I giggle.

Chapter Forty-Nine

After these revelations, I feel as if looking for a pirate treasure is anticlimactic. But we've come this far.

"CJ, where is this secret location?" Keston asks.

Kelley sweeps the paddle in the water creating blue angel wings. Keston does the same on the other side of the boat.

"This is so pretty," Tabitha exclaims. She turns to me and says, "Yes, don't keep us waiting. Where is it?"

"A cave," I say. "There's supposed to be a cave around here."

Kelley stands up and points straight ahead. "Go that way. I know where it is. Dad and I . . ." He stops and looks at Keston with stricken eyes.

"It's okay, dude," Keston says. "Tell us."

"Dad and I used to go there to fish. He said the cave was special. But he didn't say why."

Keston starts the boat. The men drop the paddles in the boat.

We chug slowly along close to the tall mangroves. An eerie feeling lingers in the air. Like when the music in a movie turns ominous. Something is about to happen.

"Stop here," Kelley says. "I haven't been here since I was fourteen, but I recognize this spot."

"Where's the cave?" I ask. I lean over the side of the boat peering into the darkness. "All I see are rocks and trees."

The only light is the blue glow of the waves when one hits the side of our boat.

"We have to drop the anchor," says Keston. "I can't get any closer."

Kelley explains that the cave is past the large boulders ahead of us.

"You have to climb over the rocks to see the cave. When the tide is in, the sea covers the beach like now. The cave is accessible only by swimming to it.

"It's easier to access when the tide is out. I haven't been here since I was fourteen. It looks the same."

"Who wants to wait until the tide goes out?" I ask.

Nobody raises their hand. "Fine, let's do this."

As Keston hauls out the anchor to throw overboard, Kelley shines a light on the rock face. "There it is. You can see the cave a little through holes in the rocks."

We all stare at the rounded cave opening tucked behind a rock face. I wonder how Keston and Kelley's father knew it was there.

I get the feeling Keston's father knew a lot more than what he told his family about. He must have known the cave was important, but did not know where the treasure was hidden.

"What's next, CJ?" Keston asks.

I open my phone. "I wrote it down. Hold on."

I find my Notes app. "I wrote out the entire secret log entry, which is too long and too sad to read now."

"No, read it," Keston urges.

"How sad?" Tabitha asks.

"What's the point of finding treasure if we don't know the story behind it." Kelley sits back down. Crosses his arms. "We have time."

"I'm warning you. It may upset you. These are real people. Your ancestors."

I don't hear any objections, so I read aloud:

December 24th, 1803

This night has been one of both profound joy and deepest sorrow. Under the eerie blue glow of phosphoric fire, I brought Charlotte, heavy with our child, to the hidden cave on the northern shore of St. Nicholas. The cave, known only to my crew and me, served as our sanctuary, its walls alive with light as if the very sea itself sought to guide our path.

We stare at the blue light flowing in and out of the cave. It looks the same as he described it on that long ago night. I continue reading.

Charlotte, ever the brave soul, faced childbirth with a courage that would put the stoutest heart to shame. Amidst the echoing sounds of the surf, she brought forth not one, but two lives into our tempestuous world. Twins they were—a boy and a girl.

"Twins!" Tabitha beams. "We have twins in our family! I didn't know it started as far back as Charlotte."

Kelley takes Tabitha's hand. "Go on, CJ."

The joy of the boy's first cry was swiftly marred by the quiet of his sister, who was born into this world only to leave it before her time. My heart, so often steeled against the cruelties of life at sea, found no armor against this grievous loss. In the quiet hours of dawn, as Charlotte rested, I took our tiny, lost daughter and laid her to rest within the cave, her eternal cradle.

"Oh," Tabitha sighs. "Poor baby."

We all look at the cave differently, knowing it is where Charlotte's and Kipson's daughter is buried. Their great ancestor.

"This is the part with the treasure," I say.

With my daughter, I placed a chest of Spanish gold, spoils from a galleon we waylaid some months past and had buried nearby. This treasure, once a symbol of victory and fortune, now marks the resting place of my child, a beacon of our love and loss. I buried them deep within the earth of the cave, under a formation that resembles the prow of a ship, as if to sail her safely to the next world. Here, in this haven, they are shielded from the world's reach, guarded by sea and stone.

"That is a symbol of a father's eternal love," Keston says.

"A bond greater than death," Kelley agrees.

Charlotte knows nothing of the gold, only that our daughter rests in a place of beauty and peace, watched over by the light of the sea. As for my son, he shall grow not knowing the weight of gold but of the depth of the ocean and the call of freedom that it sings.

This entry, penned by a hand weary with grief, is a vow—a promise that while I may roam the seas, part of me will forever remain here, in this cave, by the side of my daughter, beneath the silent watch of the glowing waters.

We sit in silence absorbing the last words.

"We can't take it," Kelley says.

Keston nods. "I agree."

Tabitha's brow furrows. "If it's still there, we need to protect it from others."

"Or we can donate it to St. Nicholas. Think of how wonderful it would be for the museum. Lots of people would visit and learn the history of your island." I smile thinking of the looks on the tourists' faces when they see the treasure.

"It sounds like there's a lot of gold and jewels. Pirate treasures are worth billions today. Our little museum won't be able to handle all of that," Keston points out.

"Let's see if it's even there first," says Kelley. "Maybe someone found it long ago. Maybe Dad found it and left a sign." His voice is young and hopeful.

"I'd like to see the treasure the Pirate King Kipson captured from those Spanish conquistadores," I add.

Keston says he doesn't care about gold and jewels.

We all look at Tabitha, who's been quiet. "This man loved my great-grandmother so much. I want to see his tribute to her and their daughter. They are my family, too."

It's agreed. Tabitha and I will stay in the boat and shine the lights while Keston and Kelley swim to the rocks, climb up and over them, then dive into the pool of water to swim to the cave.

"And don't forget," I instruct them. "You're looking for *"a formation that resembles the prow of a ship."*

"Right," says Kelley and Keston together.

"When you find that, come back, and we will wait until the tide goes back out so we can all go back together." Tabitha lays out the plan in full.

Keston kisses me goodbye before diving into the sea. He makes a bright blue splash.

"Nice, babes," I call out to him. "Be careful."

Kelley leaps next. But not before he says, "Thank you, CJ."

I can't believe this is happening. We're going to find pirate treasure. It all seems so unreal and mythical. Until I'm standing in a boat watching two brothers set out to claim their legacy.

"Do you think they'll find any treasure?" Tabitha asks.

I press a fist to my mouth. Keston is helping Kelley up on a rock. Their arms are locked together. From here it is hard to tell them apart. I hear laughter and a big splash.

"I think they've already found it."

Chapter Fifty

The sky darkens and the rain falls slanting its way under our rain jackets and hoods.

I yank up the zip on my jacket that I never leave home without anymore. Tabitha has a hoodie she's burrowing under. I throw her a tarp I find in the cubby hole. "Use this," I shout.

Rain pours into my mouth. I'm forcing myself not to think about the hurricane and the terrible rain and wind I survived just months ago.

"It will blow over," Tabitha shouts back.

"I hope so." But the sky is black and heavy. The rain pounds the boat and us like thousands of small, never-ending hammers on my head. I want to run and hide, but we're exposed.

I pray the wind doesn't pick up. It's the wind that I fear. It can be a bully picking up trees and even boats and tossing them wherever it wants.

"Please, God, no wind," I pray.

The lights we are shining on the cave are useless under the dark torrent. I hope they are safely inside the cave, protected from the storm.

Five minutes later, a terrible sound reaches our ears.

"Is that Kelley screaming?" I ask, terrified. I poke my head out of my hood.

Tabitha's eyes are bright in the darkness. "Did you hear that?" she asks, her voice shaky.

Gone is the glamorous goddess. In its place is a scared woman.

My heart freezes.

"It sounded like Keston."

She shakes her head wildly. "Or Kelley. I couldn't tell."

I shout over the rain. "Are you okay?"

No answer. Just the incessant drumming of rain on the boat and the striking of the lagoon's water.

I'm starting to breathe easier when I hear it again.

This time, the scream is blood-curdling.

It sounds like Keston. He's in pain.

Above the sound of the rain, I hear the word, "Stop!"

Tabitha grips my arm. "What are we going to do?"

I look around wildly. Keston's ever-present machete is at the side of the captain's seat. I grab it and jump into the water.

Tabitha screams, "What are you doing?"

Lord alone knows. But I must do something. That is my Keston out there.

I doggy paddle with the machete in one hand, my legs pumping away. Rain stings my eyes. The water is murky, and the luminous blue lights have disappeared.

My hood blocks my vision, so I push it back. Between the rain and the lagoon's waves, I hope I don't drown.

I finally reach the rocks. I lay the machete in a crook and pull myself up after it. I may be forty, but I'm fit from hours of treadmills and spin cycles.

Although nothing here resembles a nice cozy gym and cushy machines, which I'd kill for right now.

"Keston!" I shout at the top of my sore lungs.

"CJ!"

It's Kelley. I run in the direction of his voice. Well, not run. Crawl is more like it.

The jagged sea rocks forged by wind and waves cut my hands and knees. I've seen the island men and boys walking barefooted on rocks like these to fish or search for whelks sticking to the side of the rocks.

My walking on them is out of the question.

"Where are you?" I shout.

"Here, but don't come close."

Kelley's voice, usually cool and calm, ricochets with fear. I swallow my fear and call, "Where's Keston?"

No response. I start praying. "I'm coming." I put as much bravery into my voice as possible.

I finally reach the edge of the rocks and look over into a blue-green pool of water surrounded by more rocks. The tide is still high, so the beach is covered.

I recall Kelley's words. You have to swim through the pool to the cave during high tide.

My stomach drops. This does not look like a place for any woman to give birth. I curse Pirate Kipson in my head.

I could easily leap from my rocky outcropping to the water below. The rocks surround the pool and the entrance to the partly submerged cave.

The rocks form an amphitheater around the cave.

Kelley clings to a rock with both hands. One of his legs is leaking blood that the rain is quickly washing away.

I can't tell if he cut himself on the rocks or something else. Holding the machete above my head, I scoot my butt across the rocks. Thank God I'd changed into my jeans before leaving the villa.

"Don't come any closer," Kelley shouts. "Stay there."

"Where's Keston?" My teeth are chattering, but not from the cold. It isn't cold. It's warm, too warm for nighttime, even in the tropics. Which means a storm is brewing. I learned that on No Man's Land.

"He's in the water," Kelley's voice is weak. "He made it to the cave. "

How much blood has Kelley lost?

I peer into the water, swiping rain from my eyes, my heart in my throat.

"CJ!"

Oh my God. It's Keston. His voice is far away, as if coming from underwater.

"Babe, where are you?"

"Go home." His voice is fainter now. "It's bad."

"Don't be an ass. I'm not going home."

A sudden movement in the blue-green pool splashes water on me. It's not rain. It's not a fallen rock.

It's something large and alien-looking, and it's right below my feet.

I scream and yank my feet up. "What the fuck is that?"

Another swirl of water follows a great big splash.

I peer into the depths.

Something is twisting and turning down there.

I scream. "Is that a shark?"

"Leave," Kelley says. "It's a . . . ."

Before he can finish, the thing leaps out of the pool; its slimy green head aims for me. Its mouth opens wide, and sharp, dinosaur-looking teeth snap at my foot. The thing is huge!

About nine feet long. And wider than my body.

My legs kick out. I scramble back fast and hit my head. The machete falls out of my hand and slides on the rock. I grab it before it falls into the water.

The sea monster drops back into the pool and swirls its long green tail before disappearing.

My breath is ragged. I can't believe what just happened. I must be dreaming.

"Keston?" I cry.

Kelley is still clinging to the rock but inches his way up slowly, his right foot dragging as if broken. "Go back, CJ," he struggles to speak.

"Keston? Are you there?"

The worst thing in the world is knowing the person you love is in danger. All your adrenaline kicks in because you're not going to leave him. No way. And if you must kill a goddamn sea monster, so be it.

"What is that thing?" I shout.

"It's got to be a giant eel." Tabitha pants behind me. "A moray eel. Or a green eel. I didn't get a clear look. Those devils can bite and kill you."

She's crawling across the rocks like I did after having swam from the boat. I never thought I'd be glad to see this woman, but I am.

I point to Kelley on the rocks on the other side of the pool. "He's hurt. Keston is in the cave," I whisper, pointing to the opening you can only get to by jumping into the pool and swimming past the eel.

"Why are you whispering?" Tabitha asks.

"In case that thing can hear us."

I realize how dumb that sounds, but she didn't see the alien monster that rose out of that pool.

"Their bite is extremely painful," Tabitha says. "It looks like one bit Kelley. We must get him help."

"How many are there?" I squeal.

"They live alone or in groups. Could be more than one that's been living in this cave for a long time."

I wipe the rain from my eyes. "I must find Keston. I think he's hurt and trapped down there."

"We should go get help," says Tabitha, wiping her eyes too.

"I'm not leaving them here in the middle of the night with that monster. Plus, a storm is coming."

As if it heard me, the giant eel leaps out of the pool again. Its snake-like body is glistening with slick mucus, and its jaws open so wide we can see down its throat. Tabitha and I scream and scurry back.

"Fuck," Tabitha says. "That's the biggest eel I've ever seen."

"CJ," Keston calls. "Baby." His voice fades away. I can't hear what he's saying.

"Honey," I shout. "Hold on."

"This is impossible," Tabitha cries. "We can't help him."

"We can and we will."

I grip her shoulders. "I'm going to need your help."

She stares at me with frightened eyes. "How?"

"First, you've got to kick fear to the curb."

I give her the pep talk I gave myself when Keston and I were in danger on No Man's Land. "Fear is a big bully trying to take control. Don't let it."

She mumbles the words to herself.

"Next, I need you to focus."

She nods, still mumbling the words that fear is a bully.

"I'm going to have to take out that thing. Although I hate to do it. We're invading its home. But he's already injured Kelley and, I think, Keston, too. Now, it's coming after us. It's got to go."

"Got to go," Tabitha repeats. I worry she's in shock.

"I'm counting on you, Tabitha," I say after relaying the plan.

"I got it. I'll do it."

With the machete firmly in one hand, I step over the edge of the rocks. "Here goes."

I begin inching my way down the rocks that lead into the pool. I guess Kelley and Keston jumped in and were greeted by the beast.

I'm taking the quiet approach. Bit by bit, my feet find footholds while getting scraped raw from the rocks. My free hand holds onto the crevices for dear life.

I should have tried that rock climbing wall at the gym. Too late now.

The water is quiet below me. The eel can decide to leap out at any time and bite me in half.

I'm hoping I can surprise attack it first. It's not as smart as I am. Right?

I've got to injure it enough to give us the space and time to get out of here. The beast and his posse can have the damn treasure.

"CJ!" Kelley calls. "No."

He's inched his way to the top of his rock, blood still dripping from his leg.

"Shhh," Tabitha calls out.

When I reach almost halfway down, I find a flat crevice and plant my feet on it.

I wait. And wait. About ten minutes pass by before I sense movement in the water.

I grip the machete with all my might. My heart thumps so loudly I'm sure the monster eel can hear it.

"No fear," I mutter. "No fear."

The water parts, and the moray eel pokes its ugly head up.

"It's coming," yells Tabitha.

"Now!" I shout.

Tabitha throws rocks at the eel's head, causing it to screech and leap higher. The slimy body hangs suspended between heaven and sea. I have a full-on view of the dangerous beast.

With my feet wide apart to gain purchase on the rocks, I raise the machete above my head.

Like a character in a video game, I swing it hard, using all my body strength to slice my way through.

The machete slices through the eel's slime, its flesh, and its guts. I yank it out fast and strike another blow to its midsection.

A rush of adrenaline flows through my veins. "For Keston!" I scream at the top of my lungs.

I wield Keston's machete two more times, four in total. I twist the machete and snap it back out.

The beast's wounds are deep. How did I go from being squeamish about a fish thrown into our boat to killing a massive eel?

I doubt my stab wounds are fatal. Hopefully, the eel will dive deep down and lick its wounds somewhere far away.

All the fear I'd chased away floods my brain, and I begin to tremble. That was nuts, I mutter.

My hands and feet are soaked with blood from the eel. I tell Tabitha to throw more rocks down in case there's another one waiting in the wings. She does, but no other eel shows up.

My stomach feels queasy. I vomit on the rocks. So much for being a video game hero.

When I feel it's safe enough to go into the water, I drop off the rock ledge and swim/run to the cave's entrance.

Keston is lying in a heap right past the cave opening—blood leaks from what looks like several bite wounds.

"Honey, it's me," I croon, stroking his hair and cheeks. "It's going to be okay."

From the pallor of his face, he's lost a lot of blood. Good Lord, if these brothers are both bleeding, who will donate blood?

First things first. I help Keston to stand and move him carefully to the water.

"Look, CJ," he whispers.

I look at where he's pointing. "What is it?"

"A rock shaped like a ship's prow. The treasure must be buried under it."

I gaze around the cave at the blue lights sparkling in pools of water. At the cathedral of rocks rising to a high ceiling.

"This is where your ancestor was born—the twins. One died and was buried here. Imagine that."

"We don't need the treasure. But it's beautiful."

Keston clings to my arm. "So are you."

"Let's go home, baby."

He croaks. "To your villa?"

I shake my head, my wet curls dripping in my eyes. "No. *Your* home."

"Our home," he corrects me.

The rest of the rescue is a blur. I manage to help Keston out of the cave and up to the rock. Tabitha, meanwhile, climbs across the rocks to get Kelley.

Thinking ahead, I swam to the boat and returned with two life jackets to put around the men. After that, it was easy to tow them to the boat.

Well, not easy, but after fighting a sea monster, it seemed so.

Tabitha knows how to drive boats, so she took the wheel and got us started back down the coast, where we tied up at Keston's jetty.

Trixie met us at the jetty. Somehow, between me and Tabitha, we manage to haul one brother at a time onto Trixie's back.

Trixie happily trotted Keston to Tabitha's car and came back for Kelley. She was a lifesaver even while the tall brothers' feet hung down almost to the ground.

The hospital was a whole scene with the emergency room doctors rushing to stitch up Keston and perform minor surgery on Kelley.

They shared a room for three days and nights. By the end of their hospital stay, they were almost best friends. I say almost because Keston still insists I am his best friend.

Which I agree with.

Tabitha and I are not best friends, but we are now okay in the same room. Especially after she planned a huge book launch for Keston's Rum Cocktail book, which is turning out to be a runaway success in the resort gift shop and online.

But that comes later, after I leave for New York, and return for good to St. Nicholas with a million suitcases and two espresso machines.

Before I leave New York, my girlfriends give me a lovely send-off at my condo, which Giselle will live in until it's sold.

There were kisses, tears, hugs, and "I miss you."

"Mikah has a ticket to visit me at Christmas, which is only a couple of months away. Can you all come?"

Giselle promises she'll do her best. Lisa says she'll ask her hubby. Katana says she'll sell her firstborn if necessary, but she's not missing the trip.

"You're viral again. It's all over the internet," Mikah exclaims, sipping a cocktail I made from Keston's book.

"Yeah, CJ, you're a superhero," Katana says.

I blush furiously. "I was rescuing my boyfriend from a giant eel."

A line I never thought I'd say.

"Did you guys mark the cave so you can find it again?" asks Giselle.

I shake my head no. "We don't need to mark it. I know where it's located. But honestly, the treasure can stay where it is. We almost lost two lives trying to find it."

My friends nod solemnly.

"But just in case, you did mark it, right?" Lisa asks.

"Keston marked the location with his blood," I admit.

"A sharpie would have been better," Katana says.

I roll my eyes. "I'm happy to be alive. I still have nightmares of that green monster."

"So, what made you decide to move to St. Nicholas permanently? It wasn't the pirate treasure, since you didn't find it," says Mikah.

"Frankly, it was your words of wisdom." I poke her. "You told me I didn't have to know how things would work out. As long as I trusted myself. And I do."

"I said all that?" Mikah asks.

I nod up and down. "That and much more. I can't wait to see what happens between you and Kelley Kips."

She blushes. "Me either. We talk every day on the phone."

"I see a double wedding in our future," Lisa says with a teasing laugh.

"Don't jinx us," Mikah says.

"Right, don't."

Chapter Fifty-Two

On my first night back, Keston invited Kelley over, and we barbequed on the beach in front of our house.

It's wonderful to see them interact like siblings. Kelley has lost his wounded look, probably because of his brother's love and friendship. Keston has helped Kelley to come out of his shell.

As we eat the delicious veggie and fish kebabs Kelley grilled, Keston says, "One of the reasons I never wanted to sell any part of this land is because I believed deep down that you deserved some. I couldn't admit it to myself until recently."

"I don't want any of your land." Kelley spreads his arms outward. "Grandma Viola left it to you. It was in her Will."

Keston frowns. "Her Will said she left everything for her grandchildren. That's me, Vanessa, whose life is in England, and who says she doesn't want to return here. And *you*."

Kelley ducks his head. "It won't stand up in court. I was the illegitimate son."

"You're my brother. Who said anything about court?"

Kelley's eyes take on the glassy look of the sea on a calm day. "You don't have to do that." He takes a big swig from his flask and wipes his lips.

"I should have done it a long time ago. I'm sorry I ignored you," Keston says.

"Wasn't your fault your dad kept me a secret."

"*Our* dad."

"Yeah, right," Kelley sighs. "Our father."

"He messed up. I'd have liked to have a brother growing up."

Kelley flicks a flat beach stone across the water. It hopscotch five times. "Me too."

Keston throws his rock. It skips seven times. Kelley looks at him with admiration. "Good one, bro."

As I watch emotions race across Keston's face — sadness, anger, frustration, even despair — I realize I was waiting to discover this. Keston's constant cheerfulness hid a well of emotional darkness. Now that it's all rising to the surface, he's expressing more than joy and cheer. He's becoming complete.

With the good, the bad, and the ugly.
And I love all of him.

Later, as the brothers stir up the beach bonfire, I sense the closing of one book and, hopefully, the start of a new one.

"I made dessert," I shout, clambering up from the sand.

Kelley says, "I don't eat sugar."

"Please, dude, you're eating this."

I walk down the front steps of the house, carefully holding the coconut custard pie I made from the recipe I found in Charlotte Campbell's diary—the same pie she made to woo her pirate king hundreds of years ago.

"It's not made with *sugar*," I tell the brothers as I dole out two giant pieces. "I used real sugar cane juice. It's what Charlotte Campbell used."

Kelley sniffs his plate of pie. "Interesting. You could do a comparison test. One with sugar and this one."

Keston is diving in, not interested in discussing the difference between refined white sugar and raw sugar cane juices. "Yum," he nods appreciatively. "The best pie . . . ever."

I beam. "Thank you."

Kelley takes a big bite and chews thoughtfully. He puts down his fork. "Bro, if you don't ask her to marry you, I will."

Keston stops chewing. "You ever heard the story of Cain and Abel, bro? It didn't end well for one of those brothers."

We all laugh. It is a companionable moment. A sign of many to come, I hope.

"I'm not saying you *should* get married," Kelley sips his

dandelion wine, passing the flask to Keston. "But if I were you . . . ."

"Don't put words in his mouth, Kelley. He'll get there. In his own time." I'm blushing furiously. How awkward is this?

Keston shakes his head at me. "I've *been* there, woman. I wanted to give you space and time to decide what you wanted."

Kelley turns toward me. "The ball is in your court, CJ. Meanwhile, can I have another slice, please?"

I take my time slicing another piece of pie for Kelley.

"Um . . . well . . . he's never really asked me or anything, but . . . ."

"How do I tell the woman I love that I can't possibly love her any more than I already do? But I'm willing to give it a hundred years and a couple more generations to find out." Keston stares at me point-blank.

A moment of silence passes.

"Same!" I shout, throwing myself into Keston's arms. He wraps them around me so tightly I know he'll never let me go.

"We're in this thing together, dude," I kiss him on his coconut custard-smeared lips. "You can't get rid of me."

"Or me," Kelley laughs.

"Hee-haw!" brays a noisy donkey.

"Or Trixie," we all say at the same time.

I say a mental thank you to Charlotte Campbell, whose determination to follow her heart despite all the odds got us to this moment on the same beach where she fell in love at first sight with an African pirate king on gorgeous St. Nicholas Island.

It's our turn to carry on their legacy. I hope we can love each other as fiercely and completely as they did.

Dear Reader 🩶,

Please <u>Leave a Review</u> on Amazon to help others find this book! It can be super short. It would mean a lot to me (and to Trixie!). Thank you!

Do you wish YOU were at the Cocoa Reef Resort testing rum cocktails. Then get your **FREE** copy of Keston's **Rum Cocktail Book** 🍸 by signing up for my newsletter here —>
https://BookHip.com/VVRGKRJ

It's full of new cocktails. I made my friends taste-test them for you! As Keston would say, "You better sign up, woman!" 😄
Enjoy!

Lynn Joseph is from Trinidad & Tobago. When she's not writing her international romances, she can be found on a beach somewhere in the world. Or binge-watching *Hart of Dixie* and *The Vampire Diaries* over and over. Lynn lives in charming South Portland, Maine, and on the Caribbean Island of Tobago, where she's known as the Mermaid Queen. Join her on her journey of love, food, and romantic destinations (not necessarily in that order). www.lynnjosephbooks.com

Stay Connected

Sign up for Lynn's newsletter and receive a FREE ebook, *Princess Aboard.* Plus be in the know for all the behind the scenes goodies and more!

Sign Up Here —>
https://BookHip.com/NKSQGRS

Follow her on social media:

Facebook -http://facebook.com/lynnjosephauthor
Instagram - https://www.instagram.com/lynnjosephbooks/
Bookbub - https://bit.ly/3Phcsuu
Amazon - https://amzn.to/3VTd8Kb
Goodreads -https://bit.ly/4gUtZo4

Lynn loves to hear from her readers and invites them to email her, anytime at lynn@lynnjosephbooks.com

www.lynnjosephbooks.com

Also by Lynn Joseph

The Walker Sisters Forever Series

(Sweet Romance)

Gelato Forever

Olives Forever

Sangria Forever

Paris Forever

Christmas Forever

Cocoa Reef Resort Series

(Steamy Romance)

Lime to My Coconut

Rum to the Reggae

Spice for My Santa

Princess Abroad

(Read for FREE! —> https://BookHip.com/NKSQGRS)